BEAUTIFULLY SPUN

CANDIED CRUSH #15

CHARITY PARKERSON

—Warning: This book is intended for readers over the age of 18.

Copyright © 2021 Charity Parkerson
Editor: BZ Hercules & Consultants
ISBN: 978-1-946099-87-7
All rights reserved.

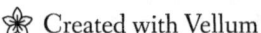

INTRODUCTION

Zayn is looking for love. Spencer wants to live the single life forever. One of them is doomed to fail.

Spencer Wright, better known as Zealous Blaze, is the number one DJ in the world. Not only does everyone know his name, he's also the most sought-after man on the scene. There's zero chance anyone is tying him down. His life is too crazy. He would be insane to let himself get ensnared by one person. It's too bad Spencer can't stop thinking about Zayn.

Zayn has the worst luck with men. He's rich and works hard on his body. Zayn would like to think he's also a nice guy. It just seems like there's no one left out there for him. Everyone he meets only wants to hook up. Zayn wants a real relationship. It doesn't help that he has his heart set on the unattainable. From the first time he set eyes on Spencer, he hasn't wanted anyone else.

Mixing tracks isn't Spencer's only talent. He also has Zayn's head completely spun out of control with the way he wants Zayn one day, and then he pushes Zayn away the next. Maybe this next time, Zayn won't come back.

ONE

MEETING MEN on dating apps was the absolute worst. Unfortunately, Zayn didn't meet men around every corner in real life. That meant Zayn was stuck with the mixed bag of crap that was online dating. Javier Bisset was a world-renowned heart surgeon. He had a good twenty years on Zayn, but he was Zayn's third date this week. Pickings were getting slim. Javier seemed nice enough, if not a little reserved. They had spoken on the phone a few times before setting up this date, and every conversation had been on the up and up before now. Still, Zayn had gone back and forth with himself about meeting Javier. In the end, he needed to give the man a shot, age difference or not.

. . .

Cool air washed over Zayn as he stepped inside the elite luncheon spot in the heart of upscale L.A. Zayn took off his sunglasses and scanned the crowd.

"Good afternoon, sir. Do you have a reservation?"

Javier came to his feet at a nearby table.

Zayn flashed the maître d' a smile. "My date is right there."

The man nodded, and Zayn headed Javier's way. Javier was tall, dark-haired, and handsome. Intelligence flashed in Javier's eyes, no doubt making people instinctively trust every confident word he spoke. That was the way of most respected doctors. A gorgeous—if not too white—smile spread across Javier's face as Zayn neared. He held out his hand for Zayn to shake.

. . .

"Zayn. It's so nice to finally meet you in person. Wow." He released Zayn's hand and touched his chin. Before Zayn grasped his intentions, Javier tilted Zayn's face from side to side, openly inspecting him. "You've taken amazing care of yourself. I took a chance on you since you're over forty. Honestly, I thought you might be a catfish or had work done, but if so, you have an amazing plastic surgeon. I'm not seeing any scars. You'll be the perfect arm candy."

For a moment, Javier shocked Zayn speechless with his audacity. Then the outrage set in. "Um. Yeah. That's going to be a no from me. Don't contact me again." Without a word, Zayn headed for the door. Despite longing to be settled down with someone he could call his, Zayn was not that fucking desperate. He made it to his car before Javier caught him.

"Zayn. Wait. I'm sorry."

Zayn took a calming breath and turned Javier's way, even though he didn't doubt he would regret it. He lifted his eyebrows and waited for Javier to say whatever he intended to say.

Javier pasted on a pained expression that looked practiced to Zayn. "Please accept my apology and come back inside. I have a problem with attracting gold diggers, which I can tell by your car you're not." Javier's gaze moved from the Chiron Zayn drove back to Zayn's face. He smiled. It was fake. "I tend to be obnoxious to weed out the weak."

Zayn barely restrained an eye roll. "You should stick with the gold diggers since your rudeness also weeds out the strong. Have a nice life."

Javier didn't give up. "I'm sincerely sorry. Please come back inside and have lunch with me. I promise you won't regret giving me another chance."

"Zayn?"

. . .

Zayn fought a wince at the sound of his name being yelled across the parking lot.

"Zayn Tanaka. I thought that was you."

Of all the people in the entire world that Zayn didn't want to see him in this position, it was Spencer Wright. Most people knew Spencer as Zealous Blaze. He was the most sought-after DJ in the entire world, and he was also the one man Zayn wanted more than he craved his next breath.

Zayn pasted on a smile that felt brittle even to him as Spencer headed his way. "Hey."

Spencer barely spared Javier a glance before his icy blue gaze landed on Zayn again. "It is a small world, dude. I literally just had coffee with Felix this morning. It's like I'm seeing his peeps all over the place. Are you leaving or going inside?"

. . .

Zayn's gaze moved between Javier and Spencer. Javier wore a cold expression that matched his flawless suit that likely cost thirty grand. Spencer looked like a Viking pimp. His light blond hair was perfectly styled, and his beard looked freshly brushed, but he was dressed like nothing Zayn had ever seen. His brown leather pants somehow went perfectly with his bare chest and fur coat. The two complete opposites stared back at him, waiting for him to answer. An unexpected and powerful desire to burst into uncontrollable laughter overwhelmed him.

A ridiculous smile pulled at Zayn's lips. "I have no idea."

"Ah. Well. It be like that sometimes." Spencer threw his arm across Zayn's shoulders and steered him to the door, leaving Javier behind as if he didn't exist. "Let me decide for you. After all, when you don't know which way you're headed, it's best to let someone else be in charge."

· · ·

Zayn couldn't stop smiling. The door to the restaurant flew open as the staff rushed to serve Spencer.

"Good afternoon, Mr. Blaze. Your usual table is occupied, but we have another waiting."

Spencer winked at Zayn before looking the maître d's way. "Thank you. This is my friend, Zayn. Let's make sure he's every bit as happy as I always am." Spencer shrugged off his coat and passed it along.

Zayn didn't notice who took it. He couldn't tear his gaze from Spencer's body. It was cut. Every muscle was perfectly defined. In the past, Zayn hadn't really gravitated toward that. Even as a part-time bodybuilder who appreciated the hard work it took to look like Spencer, muscles had never been his thing on other men. Zayn had always liked regular people, but Zayn saw a lot that he liked now because it was Spencer.

. . .

No one said a word about Spencer's shirtless state as they headed for their table. At the edge of their table, Spencer waited for Zayn to choose a seat before grabbing a chair, pulling it as close to Zayn as possible, and draping his arm over Zayn's shoulders again.

Spencer spoke to the staff while Zayn stayed lost in watching the way Spencer's jaw moved. He had met Spencer at a friend's house one time, but he had seen the guy countless times Spencer didn't know about. Zayn was a fan. He felt like a rabid one at the moment.

Finally, Spencer's gaze moved Zayn's way. It felt like they were alone inside their own bubble. Spencer smirked. "You can thank me for the rescue now."

A smile exploded across Zayn's face. "You have no idea how much I sincerely appreciate you saving me from what—undoubtably—was about to be a scene."

. . .

A loud laugh burst from Spencer. His eyes swam with good humor. Zayn couldn't stop smiling while looking at Spencer. He looked like such a happy person. The guy wore a gold chain around his neck that probably cost a hundred grand. He didn't seem to give any fucks about conforming to society. Spencer made Zayn want to be wild too. Maybe that was why Zayn had started secretly going to some of Spencer's raves. He stayed out of sight and made sure Spencer didn't spot him. Zayn could resist him. Spencer was like an untamed animal Zayn wanted to pet.

"Why did you come to my rescue?" The question was out there before Zayn could think better of it.

Their drinks arrived. Spencer didn't respond until after their server walked away and he had taken a sip of his drink. His amazing blue gaze locked on to Zayn and Zayn knew no matter Spencer's answer, it was worth the wait.

. . .

"For the same reason that I do everything. Selfishness." His gaze turned heated as it dropped to Zayn's lips. Butterflies stirred in Zayn's gut. His mouth went dry. Only God knew how often Zayn had fantasized about Spencer since they'd met. He wanted to taste Spencer's lips. In his heart, Zayn knew his flavor would be every bit as wild as he looked. Spencer's gaze moved back to Zayn's eyes. His smile returned. "What were you doing with an old guy anyhow?"

"I'm old," Zayn said without thought.

Spencer snorted. "I'm not talking about years on this earth. After all, I'm forty-six. I meant in spirit. That guy was as stiff and dusty as the crypt keeper."

An unexpected laugh burst from Zayn at the comparison even as he fought his surprise. Never in a million years would Zayn have guessed that Spencer was six years older than him. He seemed so young. "We met on a dating app and he didn't seem so bad over the phone. That's why you caught me running away. I don't mind the extra years. For me, it's all about the heart. He has an ugly one. I couldn't get away fast enough." Zayn found his gaze dropping to Spencer's mouth again. He had nice lips. They looked firm. "I'd much rather spend my time with someone fun." The confession slipped out in Zayn's distraction. It was worth it to witness the way Spencer's lips turned up in one corner in a sexy smirk.

Spencer handed him a menu. "You should try the shrimp and calamari. It's amazing. You'll need your strength."

Zayn accepted the menu, proving his body could still work with a frozen brain. There was no missing the sexual innuendo or the spark between them. He wasn't the type to sleep around recklessly, but there was no way he would turn Spencer down. No matter how this lunch ended, Zayn was onboard. He wanted more of Spencer. Zayn craved everything.

Zayn Tanaka was a name everyone knew. If they said otherwise, they were lying. Zayn was the creator of the biggest crypto currency in the world. He was worth so much money, he had literally made his life worthless. From what Spencer understood from their mutual friends, Felix and Koda, Zayn was a part time bodybuilder because he had nothing at all to do but exist. He could live a thousand lazy and extravagant lifetimes on his money and still never go broke. To anyone else, that might sound amazing. Spencer thought it sounded like a nightmare. He couldn't imagine living a pointless life where everyone he met wanted his wealth. Even though Spencer had money too, his life was nothing like that.

Spencer was a free spirit. He didn't give any fucks what people thought. Music was everything to him. He lived in his own world inside his head where the music played twenty-four seven. Maybe that sounded insane to anyone else, and perhaps he was a bit mad. There were worse things than insanity. He could have an old, stiff crypt keeper chasing him through the parking lot like Zayn had. Spencer smiled at his thoughts. No one would catch him growing old.

. . .

"I have to know. What's that smile about?"

At Zayn's question, Spencer's gaze slid his way. Zayn's naturally light brown tone looked even more gorgeous with the sun from the window washing over him. His brown eyes were like whiskey. Beautiful. Spencer always got what he wanted. He wanted Zayn. "I was imagining what your expression would be if I told you to take me back to your place."

A smile exploded across Zayn's face. "You think I'm pretty weak, don't you?"

That one threw Spencer off balance. "I…"

"Because I am today," Zayn said, shocking him speechless. "You should come home with me."

. . .

Spencer found himself backpedaling in the face of Zayn's unquestioning willingness. "We should eat first so I can get to know you."

Zayn shrugged. "If that's what you want. You know my name and what I do. I'm forty and boring as hell. My grandparents immigrated from Kyoto when my mom was a teenager. She married my dad a little less than two years later. They had me and promptly divorced. My mom and Koda's mom are best friends, so Koda and I grew up together. He's ten years younger than me, so we didn't really start hanging out as friends until about five years ago. I do part-time bodybuilding for competitions." He paused as if trying to find anything else to say. "I collect cars," he added, as if really digging for anything he forgot. Finally, Zayn shrugged. "That's really about it. Like I said, I'm boring."

Spencer had to admit that was more than he usually knew about anyone he slept with. "So we should go, then."

. . .

Zayn's gaze dropped to Spencer's mouth, making his stomach quiver. "I think that's best."

Without another word, Spencer stood. He dropped three hundred dollars on the table and headed for the door. No one asked questions; they simply scrambled to give Spencer back his coat. He didn't bother putting it on. It wasn't cold. Spencer had only thrown it on because he hadn't wanted to find a shirt. Sometimes, his mind jumped around too much. He had been working on a new mix when hunger struck. With no thought to anything but food, he had grabbed the first coat he saw and headed out. He hadn't expected Zayn. Zayn was another impulsive move.

Spencer had suggested Zayn's house because he had seen the guy's car earlier. He didn't imagine Zayn's would be willing to leave his nearly four-million-dollar car in the parking lot to come home with Spencer. Spencer could have suggested Zayn follow him. That option gave Zayn too much time to change his mind. Spencer would leave his Navigator. No big deal. He headed toward the passenger side of Zayn's car with the confidence of a man who knew his mind. Spencer fucked a lot of people without looking back. Zayn looked like a man who was the same. People like them didn't need anyone else for any other reason.

The car door unlocked, and Spencer slid inside as Zayn slid behind the wheel. Spencer automatically leaned Zayn's way as Zayn backed from the parking space. Zayn's shoulders were wide. He put off a warmth Spencer wanted to feel against his skin. Spencer twiddled his thumbs restlessly beneath the coat in his lap. The music pouring from the speakers had his mind slipping away, matching downbeats with a different song he had heard earlier in the day. Before that moment, he hadn't considered overlapping the two. Damn, they would sound great together. He would add that to his list when he got home. Spencer had no concept of time when his creative juices flowed. Zayn pulled into a driveway and a private gate opened automatically. He followed the drive until he circled a massive estate and into an equally large garage. They were met with an extensive car collection. It was an impressive show of wealth.

Spencer barely spared any of it a glance. He was here for the sex.

As Spencer jumped from the car, he left his coat behind. They likely wouldn't be here long. Zayn quietly waited to escort him inside. They fell into step beside each other. Still, neither of them spoke. The silence didn't bother Spencer. He didn't spend a lot of time with people. Maybe that wasn't entirely true. Spencer spent a great deal of his time at parties, raves, and clubs. He didn't think that counted. Despite always being surrounded by people, Spencer was still alone. He lived inside his mind. Everything and everyone else were just noise.

Zayn cut through the garage and into a room that was obviously part of the pool house. Windows surrounded them, and all Spencer could see was the custom pool with its waterfalls and palm trees. Zayn passed through another door and they were inside a mud room. It hit Spencer that everything was connected. There weren't any separate buildings. He supposed that was a security thing. Spencer wondered if Zayn's vast fortune limited his life. It was possible Zayn lived in constant danger. He hadn't noticed the guy needing bodyguards or anything. Spencer had spotted a few security guards since stepping onto the property, though. That discovery finally unglued his tongue.

"How often do you have people sneaking onto your property?"

Zayn flashed him a smile. "Almost daily. My security team stays busy."

Spencer still didn't pay any attention to his surroundings as they moved into the kitchen. "But you walk around freely. I've never seen you with a bodyguard."

"I've never seen you with one either." He snagged Spencer's waist and invaded his space. "And you're pretty famous."

. . .

"No one knows my face unless they know my face." Spencer hoped the explanation made sense. His brain stopped functioning properly when Zayn's body collided with his.

"Same. People recognize my name, but they don't really know my face. I don't do a lot of interviews or anything like that. Mostly, I make money and stay out of the way."

"I make beats and stay in my head."

Zayn stared at Spencer's mouth. "I've noticed that about you. You keep your eyes on your work while everyone else focuses on partying."

Zayn's claim shook Spencer from the spell his heated gaze weaved. "How many of my events have you been to?"

. . .

Zayn backed Spencer against a wall, making him realize Zayn had been steering him in that direction. Without even looking, Zayn reached up and pushed, and a panel opened behind him. They were inside a bedroom. "I've seen you enough times to appreciate your passion," Zayn answered, as if nothing happened.

Spencer glanced around. The bedroom was the size of a large theater. As the panel swung closed, Spencer realized it was a bookshelf on the other side. Zayn had an actual secret passageway into his bedroom. Spencer hadn't expected to be impressed by anything Zayn's money could buy, but he liked that. He was also completely distracted by his surroundings now. If anyone asked him to describe what he thought a billionaire's bedroom looked like, he couldn't have dreamed up this. Spencer's bedroom told a story. The passageway bookshelf had priceless comic books encased on the shelves. A miniature fantasyland of castles and dragons took up an entire corner. Meanwhile, a massive whirling light show of custom computers, screens, and keyboards filled another space. A wall-size TV took up an area by the bed. There was another mini kitchen inside the bedroom. He could see a bathroom through an open doorway. Spencer didn't know where to look first.

He finally just picked a spot. Spencer motioned toward the miniature fantasyland. "Did you build that?"

Zayn barely spared the impressive piece a glance. "Yes. I have a lot of spare time. Would you like something to drink?"

Spencer lost interest in his surroundings again. "Actually, I'd like for you to fuck me."

"That I can do." That was all the warning Zayn gave before he overcame Spencer. His mouth covered Spencer's and Spencer went from mildly interested to on fire. Even though Zayn always watched Spencer with the heat of seven suns, Zayn didn't strike Spencer as an overly passionate person. He didn't speak on any subject ardently. The guy just seemed slightly indifferent in everything. Even Zayn openly claimed he was boring. Apparently, there was one thing he did with hot-blooded enthusiasm. Spencer was all systems go. He tugged at Zayn's shirt until he had him out of it. Everything about Zayn was hard and sexy, but he also had a layer of softness Spencer hadn't been expecting. As Zayn kissed and bit at Spencer's throat and worked on unbuttoning Spencer's pants, Spencer ran his hands over every place he could reach. With his eyes closed, he savored the sensations around him. He liked to lose control. Spencer craved the feeling of being caught in a storm. He loved when the wind whipped around him, carrying him where it wanted to go. Zayn was like that. He tugged and pulled until Spencer found himself face down on an extremely plush mattress. It smelled like lavender. Spencer inhaled even as wet fingers stretched his asshole and teeth sank into his back. He moved restlessly against the mattress, wanting the pleasure his body demanded.

Spencer felt the same way he did while high. He heard the faint crinkle of a condom wrapper, then felt the blunt stretch. A laugh of pure joy burbled in his throat as Zayn forced Spencer's hips into position and pounded. It was perfect. Age and experience were a good thing. Zayn used his expertise to get his pleasure while also punching that button Spencer loved so much. Spencer didn't focus on anything other than the building tension. He let Zayn set the pace. The noises coming from his throat were beyond his control. His entire body tensed. Spencer held his breath. Zayn pulled out and flipped Spencer onto his back, tearing a cry of denial from Spencer. Before Spencer could curse him, Spencer's dick was in Zayn's mouth. Zayn sucked, pulling Spencer's waiting orgasm from him without warning. Spencer cried out and held Zayn's hair in a death grip as he rode Zayn's tongue. Zayn swallowed every drop before pushing Spencer's thighs apart and impaling him once more.

Spencer clutched the bedding and held on. All he could do was gasp as an ecstasy he had never known before rocked his soul. Zayn looked severe as he took his pleasure from Spencer's body. When Zayn blew, he whispered Spencer's name while never once breaking eye contact. Zayn melted into Spencer, claiming his mouth once more. This time, their kiss was sweet. Spencer felt a spark of something he didn't understand. He could taste his cum on Zayn's tongue. Spencer didn't want the kiss to end. He felt oddly connected to life in that moment.

When Zayn rolled away, Spencer immediately went cold. He almost jumped from the bed while Zayn tossed the condom in the trash, but then he was back. Spencer found himself squashed beneath Zayn's wide chest. His breath left him as their tongues met. Spencer couldn't completely close his eyes this time. Zayn's face fascinated him too much. It was too gorgeous. He had a crazy feeling he would be back for more. This had been an unexpected and amazing experience. All Spencer had wanted was a good time for one night. Now he wasn't so sure.

TWO

THE ROOM WAS EMPTY. Zayn didn't bother searching. He knew Spencer was gone the moment he opened his eyes. It wasn't like Zayn to fall asleep immediately after sex, but Spencer had been in his arms and his chest felt full. He had just sort of drifted away. Now Zayn was scared to move. He knew once he let consciousness take hold, he would have to face the reality of Spencer leaving. That hurt. It shouldn't. Zayn recognized Spencer only wanted sex. He wasn't an idiot, but he had seen his chance and taken it.

From the first hint of having Spencer, Zayn had been ready to go. His big brain had fled the scene and his little one had taken charge. He had seen the opportunity to touch his biggest obsession and taken it. Zayn hadn't stopped to consider the stupidity of such a thing. He should have taken his time. Played his cards right. If Zayn had moved slower, Spencer might not have sneaked away after the first time Zayn touched him. Fuck. It had been amazing, though. He could still smell Spencer's cologne. He couldn't let Spencer get away like this. Everyone used Zayn. For once, it wasn't about money. Zayn didn't know how to feel.

A thought hit and Zayn shot from the bed. He nearly tripped over his feet while trying to pull on a pair of shorts and get out the door. Zayn passed two guards on the way to the garage. No one spoke. He damn near ran the last few feet to his car. Spencer's coat was still inside. A smile that felt wicked even to him pulled at his lips. Spencer hadn't gotten away yet.

Zayn headed back to his bedroom, moving a little slower. This time, he smiled as he passed the set of guards. Hope wasn't lost yet. Zayn found his phone in the pocket of his jeans on the floor. He called Koda without a second thought.

Koda answered on the third ring. "Hello?"

"Hey, Koda. It's Zayn."

He could hear the smile in Koda's voice when he responded. "Hey, Zayn. How's it going?"

"Good. Good." Zayn had no idea why he repeated himself. He simply didn't want to sound too desperate. "Hey, so, is there any way you can find out Spencer's address for me? We had lunch earlier, and he left his coat in my car. Since I'm still out and about, I figured I would drop it by his place before I forget."

Koda's son Liam babbled in the background, letting Zayn know Koda was likely too busy for this.

Thankfully, Koda didn't let him down. "Yeah. Just give me a few. I'll call Felix at work and ask."

Zayn fought hard to keep his voice level. "Thanks. You know me. If I don't do it now, I likely won't remember later."

"No problem. Give me like five minutes."

"Sounds good. Talk to you soon."

"Bye," Koda said, disconnecting their call.

Zayn paced the floor as he waited. It was possible Felix didn't know Spencer's address. It was equally possible Felix wouldn't give the information to Zayn, even if he knew it. All Zayn could do was hope. The phone finally vibrated in his hand.

Koda: 3421 *Water Street.*

. . .

Zayn blinked at the address. Water Street was in the warehouse district. There weren't any homes in that area. Koda had gotten the address for him. Zayn didn't want to accuse Koda of being wrong, so he simply dressed and headed out. If he got there and it wasn't Spencer's place, Zayn would call Koda back. Otherwise, he needed to take a chance.

It took Zayn half an hour with traffic to get to the address in Koda's text. It was a warehouse. The parking lot was empty and there wasn't a public entrance. Instead, the place had two huge bay doors and a metal door. Zayn parked near the metal door and climbed from the car with Spencer's coat. As he reached the door, Zayn second-guessed himself and turned around. This likely wasn't Spencer's place, and he didn't think knocking would get him anywhere. Before he made it back to his car, the door swung wide.

"Yo, Zayn."

. . .

Zayn spun back toward the door. Spencer stood in the open doorway. A pair of black sweatpants rode low on his hips, exposing a set of sexy obliques. There was a hickey on his collarbone that was one-hundred-percent Zayn's fault. Zayn wanted to do it again. Then he remembered Spencer had sneaked away.

He held up the coat. "I'm not stalking you. You left your coat in my car."

Spencer's eyes flashed with humor. "Yeah. You don't strike me as the stalking type. Would you like to come in?"

Yes. He absolutely wanted to come in, but—again—Spencer had sneaked away. "Uh." Zayn rubbed the back of his neck.

Spencer snorted. "Dude. Come in."

. . .

Zayn clutched Spencer's coat to his chest and followed him inside. His jaw nearly dropped when he stepped through the door. It looked as if Spencer had transformed the place into a massive studio apartment. There was an area for a living room—like a TV and such. Another zone of the warehouse had a huge bed and racks of clothes. There was a small kitchen and a gigantic dance floor—like Spencer hosted parties here. His DJ area was surrounded by speakers and the wall had been spray-painted from one end to the other with various tags. At the bay doors, there was a huge box truck—likely for transporting rave gear and Spencer's navigator. Zayn had no words.

"I saw you pull up on the camera," Spencer said, pointing toward a nearby screen, showing the parking lot.

Zayn spared the security monitor a passing glance. "Where would you like this coat?"

. . .

Spencer shrugged as he plopped down on the couch. "Just toss it somewhere."

After draping the coat over the arm of the couch, Zayn gingerly sat. He was still unsure of his welcome. Not to mention, reeling from the sight of where Spencer lived. He knew the guy got paid an ass-ton to party for a living, but he was also in his forties. It seemed odd as hell that he lived like this.

A bark of laughter burst from Spencer. "You should see your face. Some of us don't value possessions as much as you do."

Zayn fought a wave of insult and embarrassment. He honestly didn't know where to start. "There were a lot of assumptions in that claim."

"Are you saying you don't value money?" Spencer shot back.

. . .

"Of course I care about something I worked my ass off to get, but you're assuming I have opinions on what you value. I don't. You haven't told me yet what's important to you."

Spencer cocked his head to one side and eyed Zayn. "Then why do you look so horrified right now?"

Zayn couldn't hold back. "You have two vehicles parked in the same area where you sleep. Haven't you heard of carbon monoxide?"

Spencer threw his head back, laughing. Hunger gnawed at Zayn's gut as he stared at Spencer's exposed throat. He hadn't realized he had a thing for necks until he met Spencer. Fuck, he was sexy. Spencer swiped at his eyes.

"You're funny. Like, I figured you were probably smart as fuck, but you're pretty freaking hilarious too. I'm glad you came by."

. . .

Zayn didn't know if that was a preface to asking Zayn to leave, so he rushed to secure seeing Spencer again. "You should give me your number."

Spencer sat forward and grabbed a notebook and pen from the table. He scratched out his number and passed the notebook Zayn's way. "Same."

Zayn tore out the area with Spencer's number and pocketed it before writing his down.

"I don't normally like bodybuilders. Too much muscle just isn't to my taste." Zayn glanced up at Spencer's remark. He didn't know whether to be insulted. Luckily, Spencer didn't leave his statement hanging there unexplained. "Your body is nice, though." He seemed to realize how he sounded and rushed to fix it. "I mean, usually bodybuilders are like cuddling with marble. You're not like that."

Zayn's cheeks hurt from smiling as he watched Spencer scramble to remove his foot from his mouth.

He made a dismissive gesture, wiping away Spencer's concerns. "I get what you're saying. I'm not currently cutting for any competitions, so I'm not as solid right now. Truthfully, I'll probably stay like I am. I'm losing interest in the whole competition thing. Since I've already won a few trophies, it seems pointless." Zayn blew out a sigh. He was tired just listening to himself. "Actually, I'm like this. Things don't hold my interest forever. I pick up hobbies and then run with them until I've taken it as far as I can go. Then I'm bored with it. I've been over the bodybuilding thing for a while now. I'm ready to try something new." Zayn glanced at the notebook, feeling exposed. He was unhappy. It was scary how close he had come to admitting that.

"Hey, man. Whose bad-ass car is that out front?" The words trailed off as the brown-haired guy burst through the door—like he lived there. "Oh."

Zayn dropped the notebook on the coffee table and came to his feet. "You have company. I should go."

. . .

Spencer eyed him, wearing an unreadable expression. He motioned the new arrival's way. "This is my sound guy, Jinx. Jinx, this is Zayn."

Zayn closed the distance between them and held out his hand. "Nice to meet you."

Jinx shook his hand, but his gaze moved between Zayn and Spencer. "You too." Despite his upbeat tone, Zayn recognized the jealousy in his eyes. He had made a mistake by coming here. Spencer's jacket had been safely returned. They'd had an amazing afternoon. Spencer was obviously not interested. Zayn wouldn't call.

Zayn cast a quick glance Spencer's way, hoping it wouldn't sting. "I'll let you two get to work or whatever." Without waiting for Spencer to respond, Zayn ducked out before he made a bigger fool of himself. He made it to his car before Spencer caught up with him.

. . .

"Are you really leaving without a proper goodbye?"

Zayn turned, ready to laugh off the moment. Spencer's body collided with his and heat exploded through Zayn. Before he knew it would happen, Zayn had Spencer boxed in against the car. He held Spencer's jaw and took the kiss he wanted. By the time he pulled away, they were panting.

"That's more like it." Despite Spencer's obvious attempt at nonchalance, his words sounded breathless.

"Don't lose my number."

Spencer snagged Zayn's shirt before he could get away. "I have a party out in the desert. Come. The host just puts the word out and whoever shows, shows. Come out to Hollinger Point. You can't miss it."

· · ·

Zayn didn't know if his heart could take it, but the day was young. "I'll be there." Maybe Zayn would go. He wasn't sure yet. All he knew was, he really liked Spencer. He wanted to believe they had a chance, and he was the king of fooling himself.

Spencer tried not to smile like an idiot as he headed back inside. He wasn't one to chase a dude, but damn. There was a definite spark. Spencer wanted to go back for seconds. He hadn't quite had his fill yet.

"What was that all about?"

At Jinx's question, Spencer avoided his gaze as he crossed the room. "Saying goodbye to a friend."

Jinx didn't let it go. "Uh, no. You practically ran after the guy. I've never seen that happen."

. . .

Spencer glanced at the notebook. Zayn's number was gone. "I'm a nice guy. What happened to the number on this notebook?"

"What number?"

Jinx sounded a little too guilty for Spencer's liking. "What did you do?"

Jinx shifted from one foot to the other. His light blue gaze slid past Spencer—like he couldn't look him in the eye. "I didn't pay any attention to what was written on it, but I tore a piece of paper out of your notebook to spit out my gum." He pulled the wadded paper from his pocket and tried prying it open.

Spencer ran his tongue over his teeth as he watched, fighting back his anger. Jinx had been his sound guy for about five years. He helped Spencer set up for every show. Spencer paid him good money to be there. Lately, he had been acting weird and Spencer didn't like it.

. . .

"What in the hell is going on with you?" The question burst from Spencer before he could call it back. Even to his ears, he sounded enraged.

Jinx's motions turned nervous, making Spencer immediately feel like shit. "I just wasn't paying attention. I'm sorry. Look, I didn't ruin the number part." He tried smoothing the page out on the table while tearing away the gummy mess. "I didn't mean to fuck up anything."

Spencer ran his hand through his hair and took the crinkled paper from Jinx. "It's fine. I shouldn't have snapped at you. Let's just get loaded up for the night."

With his head down, Jinx gave him a quick nod and headed for the truck. While Jinx opened the back, Spencer quickly programmed Zayn's number into his phone before anything else happened to it. With his temper ebbing, the guilt set in. Jinx had a lot going on in his life. He didn't need Spencer yelling at him. Before Spencer, very few people had given Jinx as many chances as Spencer, since Jinx had to miss a lot of work to take care of his mother. Spencer genuinely liked him. He also hated losing his cool. For a few minutes, Spencer watched Jinx load speakers into the truck. The guy was over twenty years younger than Spencer, and he looked even younger than that. Today, he moved like an old man, as if Spencer's anger sapped the life from him. That thought made Spencer feel like shit. He moved to help Jinx carry one of the biggest speakers. Jinx was strong for his lanky size, but he was still a tiny guy.

Spencer grabbed one end and lifted. "Tell me about your day. How's your mom?"

Jinx's shoulders seemed to relax. "She's okay, all things considered. We went to lunch and then went to visit my grandma. Both of them asked about you."

"I'll have to send them flowers."

. . .

Jinx didn't seem charmed by the idea. "Great." The sarcasm was thick.

Since Spencer knew when he couldn't win, he stopped trying. Instead, his thoughts drifted back to Zayn. Something about Jinx showing up had sent Zayn running. He doubted it was jealousy since Jinx was obviously an employee. Maybe he had just seen his chance to escape. After all, he had brought Spencer's coat back. All ties were cut now. There was no need to see each other again.

With the speaker loaded, Spencer walked away from the truck and dug out his phone again. He didn't like the idea of Zayn getting away.

Spencer: *Don't forget. Hollinger Point.*

The phone immediately shook in his hand before Spencer could put it away again.

. . .

Zayn: *I'll be there.*

A smile tugged at Spencer's lips. To his mind, sex with Zayn still counted as a one-night stand if it was twice in the same day. He wasn't finished with Zayn yet. Spencer couldn't wait to see him again. He refused to look too closely at why. Sometimes he couldn't control his impulses. Spencer would chalk it up to that. No reason to make this out as more. No reason at all.

THREE

FROM EXPERIENCE, Zayn knew not to leave for the rave until well after midnight. Otherwise, he would be waiting all night for the party to end and he would have a much harder time getting close to Spencer. It took Zayn twenty minutes to find a place to park and another ten to walk to where the crowd jumped in unison to the music blaring from the speakers. The only lights were the ones erected on either side of the small stage where Spencer stood, looking like a god. Otherwise, only neon glow sticks, flashing necklaces, and glowing teeth lit up the crowd. The place was surprisingly bright.

. . .

People danced and openly made out. Zayn weaved through the throng, trying his best to get as close to Spencer as possible. A cloud of pot smoke lingered in the air, making Zayn lightheaded. The closer Zayn got to Spencer, the more mesmerized he became. He was shirtless and sweat glistened on his skin. His entire body moved to the music. Muscles flexed, getting a workout, and reminding Zayn exactly what that body could do. He still couldn't believe he had made love to Spencer. For months, he had been secretly following all the raves online and showing up to watch Spencer just like this—like a stalker. Spencer lifted his chin. His gaze scanned the crowd, landing on Zayn. It didn't budge. Spencer's mouth lifted in one corner. His body kept moving to the music. Zayn's mouth went dry. The way he craved having Spencer moving like that while straddling his hips was almost a sickness. Spencer was exactly like the smoke hanging in the air. The slightest sample had him higher than he had ever been. Unfortunately, Zayn had a bad feeling that Spencer would be every bit as hard to hold on to.

A motion from the corner of his eye had Zayn looking away. Zayn spotted Jinx waving at him. Jinx leaned over and whispered in the ear of a guy built like a bull. The man's eyes locked on to Zayn. For a moment, considering the jealousy he had seen in Jinx's stare earlier, he wondered if Jinx asked the guy to send Zayn on his way. The guy nodded at whatever Jinx said and then dove into the crowd. People cleared a path.

When he reached Zayn, he leaned in and yelled against Zayn's ear, "Come on. You can sit with Jinx while Zealous finishes up."

Despite his surprise over the offer, Zayn nodded and followed the security guard through the crowd. A set of makeshift steps led into the back of Spencer's box truck. There were four folding chairs inside. Jinx sat in one. The other was occupied by a face Zayn would recognize anywhere. He imagined everyone knew Hudson Vincent. As the lead singer of a boy band, Hudson had grown up in front of the world. He had gone on to have a successful career in alt rock and was basically the king of grunge music.

. . .

Zayn climbed the steps and into the back of the truck. The sound of the party raging outside muted like magic. "Holy shit. It's way quieter in here."

Jinx tapped the wall beside him. "Betsy has soundproof lining. Plus, the speakers are set up where they won't blast into the truck. It's the only way to keep your sanity when this is your life."

Zayn imagined that was true. Partying now and then was one thing. This being a job was another. Zayn's gaze slid Hudson's way. It was out of his control. His lip and nose were pierced and his eyes were heavily lined. He had his chair leaned back on two legs while he eyed Zayn with open curiosity.

Zayn held out his hand. "Zayn."

Hudson dropped his chair back to all fours and leaned forward to shake Zayn's hand. "Hudson. Jinx was just telling me about you. So you're the famous Zayn Tanaka. What's that like?"

. . .

"Oddly boring," Zayn said, snagging one of the empty chairs for himself.

A low chuckle rumbled from Hudson. "I'm sure."

Jinx's gaze locked on to Hudson as if a thought hit him.

"What's it like to be famous?"

Hudson nodded Spencer's way. "Why not ask your friend, Zealous? I'm sure he can explain it better than I can."

Jinx shook his head. "He doesn't see himself as famous. Zealous only sees himself as blessed. You're different. There's nowhere you can go where people don't know your name."

. . .

Zayn found himself sucked into the conversation. Jinx's claim made so much sense. He could see Spencer uncaring of the fame. Zayn was also dying to hear Hudson's answer. Everyone knew Zayn's name, but he wasn't like Hudson. Likely, Hudson couldn't go anywhere without being mobbed.

For a moment, Hudson looked thoughtful, as if he didn't want to answer Jinx, or he took the question to heart. Then Hudson met Jinx's stare with a seriousness that fascinated Zayn. "Have you ever had a friend who you really liked and would do anything for, but you knew if you ever stopped skating a super thin line around them, then they would turn on you like a pack of rabid dogs in a heartbeat?"

Jinx's gaze slid away. Zayn followed his stare. It was locked on Spencer. "Yeah. I know someone like that."

Hudson tilted his chair back onto two legs and buried his hands in the pockets of his black hoodie. "Everyone is like that when you're me."

. . .

Zayn's throat swelled as his gaze automatically moved Spencer's way. He watched Spencer entertain the crowd. Jinx had known Spencer for much longer than Zayn. He would know better than Zayn if Spencer was the type to turn cold in an instant. Zayn didn't know how to feel. On one hand, he wondered if he should leave now before he got hurt. On the other, Zayn already couldn't stay away. It was possible he was too late to avoid the pain. He also didn't want to.

Music thumped in Spencer's ears. His head spun from the secondhand smoke floating around him. Even though they were outside, there were so many different drugs being smoked that Spencer didn't stand a chance. Plus, someone had passed him a pill earlier and Spencer had downed it without a single thought. Sometimes, the nights were long, and he was dumb like that.

. . .

Someone slipped Spencer their number. He barely spared the guy a passing smile before pretending to pocket the card. The moment the guy turned away, he tossed it in the trash. Zayn was nearby. Spencer wouldn't be going home with anyone else.

For the millionth time, Spencer's gaze slid toward the back of the box truck. Security kept the men inside safe. As Spencer looked on, Zayn laughed at something Hudson said. An unexpected wave of irritation washed over Spencer. He chalked it up to impatience. It was nearing three in the morning and Spencer had been at the helm since ten. He slowed things down and switched on the microphone. Things were winding down. Spencer was ready to steal Zayn away before Hudson charmed him too much.

"Enjoy this last song as you make your way to your tents and cars. It's been a blast partying with you tonight, but it's time for me to go. If you had fun, then don't forget your host. Check out Hudson's latest album, *Social Limit,* online or wherever your favorite music is sold." Spencer turned off his mic.

His gaze slid Zayn's way again. To his surprise, Zayn stood inside the open doorway of the truck, watching Spencer. Hunger sideswiped Spencer from nowhere. Zayn's muscular arms were crossed, and one sexy shoulder leaned against the wall of the truck. Spencer couldn't believe this man had been fucking him just over twelve hours earlier. Zayn patiently waited for Spencer, as if he fully intended to have Spencer again. Just the thought of being alone with Zayn had goosebumps rising on Spencer's skin. He imagined countless men had seen Zayn look at them the way Zayn stared at Spencer now, but Spencer had his attention for the moment. He fully intended to exploit the situation.

The song ended, and Spencer closed his laptop and unplugged it. Everything else could stay behind for Jinx to haul away, but his laptop always left with him. Spencer tucked it under his arm as he headed Zayn's way. He stopped at the edge of the steps and looked up. Zayn stared down at Spencer, as if waiting for Spencer to tell him their next move.

. . .

Jinx leapt from the back and started breaking down equipment.

Spencer glanced Jinx's way before meeting Zayn's stare again. "I have to get all this stuff loaded."

Zayn straightened away from the truck. "I'll help."

Hudson slapped Zayn's shoulder and squeezed. "I'll help Jinx. You two can head out. We got this."

Zayn looked between everyone. "Are you sure? That seems like a lot."

Spencer stepped in. "They're good. Jinx is the best at what he does."

Even though Zayn still didn't look comfortable leaving the pair, he jumped down and joined Spencer on the ground. Spencer inhaled Zayn's cologne. His body stirred as images of Zayn biting his skin invaded his head. A repeat performance was definitely on Spencer's agenda.

"I'm parked this way," Zayn said, motioning to their left. "I brought my Hummer since I didn't figure bringing the Chiron to the middle of the desert would be a good idea."

Spencer nodded as they fell into step beside each other. "True. Half these people are high as fuck too," Spencer said, eyeing the crowd that still lingered. "You don't want to risk any of them hitting your car."

"I'm guessing you're probably high as a kite too after inhaling that smoke all night." Before Spencer had time to respond, Zayn glanced behind him. "Are you sure we should leave Jinx and Hudson with all that work?"

A bark of laughter burst from Spencer. He linked his arm through Zayn's and kept the guy moving. "First off, a majority of what you see is set up by a staging company Hudson hired. Only some smaller speakers and equipment are mine. Second, Jinx is young and hot, and Hudson never left his side all night. This was Hudson's party. He had countless, and I do mean countless willing bodies in that crowd, yet he stayed with Jinx. It's definitely time for us to move along so Hudson can shoot his shot."

He felt Zayn relax. "Oh. I was cock-blocking all night and didn't even know it."

The laughter in Zayn's voice made Spencer smile. "Yeah, well, you and fifteen hundred other people. While Hudson is known for being pretty wild, he's not the type to fuck anyone in public while promoting a new album. His reputation is pretty important to him." Spencer glanced around. Things were thinning out quickly. "They'll be alone soon enough."

"Yo, sick beats tonight."

. . .

Spencer nodded at the guy who yelled the praise.

Zayn's hold tightened on Spencer. "Speaking of being alone with someone sexy, I'm looking pretty forward to that myself," Zayn said as they reached the passenger side of a black Hummer. The lights flashed and Zayn opened the door for him. Spencer barely spared the vehicle a glance as he climbed inside. He couldn't make himself stop holding Zayn's stare. No one had ever looked at him the way Zayn did. There was something in Zayn's eyes. It was more than desire. Spencer couldn't put a name to it. All he knew was he needed Zayn to unleash whatever he barely kept restrained when he looked at Spencer. There was a spark. Zayn wanted to burn.

When Zayn climbed behind the wheel, Spencer lost his grip on his self-control. He grabbed Zayn's shirt and hauled Zayn his way. Their mouths clashed. The light inside the vehicle dimmed until they were plunged into darkness. There were no streetlights in the desert. Only the moon and stars gave any light at all. They were alone in their cocoon of darkness and heat. Spencer massaged his way down Zayn's chest until he reached the hard-on straining against Zayn's jeans. He fought to unbutton Zayn's pants, but the angle made it impossible.

Zayn pulled away. "Give me a second."

Before Spencer could question Zayn, Zayn jumped from the vehicle and opened the back. Spencer fought to catch his breath while Zayn crawled around inside.

"Come back here."

Spencer glanced over his shoulder and the entire back rows were folded down, creating a comfy-looking bed. He didn't think twice before dumping his laptop on the floorboard and crawling between the seats. He overcame Zayn the moment Zayn reached for him. Their tongues stroked as Spencer tumbled Zayn onto his back and went to work on his clothes. They were an inferno of passion. Spencer had never felt like this before. He understood lust. This was different. It was explosive. Spencer felt like he would tear off his skin if he didn't find a way to get closer to Zayn. He barely had Zayn's erection free before he had it in his mouth. Spencer licked and sucked, reveling in the sounds Zayn made. He had a nice cock. It wasn't too big or too small. It fit perfectly inside Spencer without hurting him and made for a great meal. There were no practiced skills being used tonight. Spencer was starved, and he went wild. He pried Zayn's jeans down his hips and then two-handed Zayn's dick while sucking the tip. Zayn pulled his hair, making his scalp sting. Spencer punished him by swallowing his cock while massaging his balls.

"Oh my god, Spencer. I'm about to blow."

Spencer laughed around Zayn's shaft. He wanted it. Spencer needed Zayn's cum. A loud, erratic panting filled the inside of the car. Zayn's hips lifted, straining against Spencer's mouth. Spencer pumped and bobbed, trying to suck Zayn dry. A muffled cry reverberated from the walls of the vehicle. Hot cum filled Spencer's mouth. A moan rose in Spencer's throat. He swallowed it along with his prize. Spencer kept sucking, trying to get more. In a flash, he found himself dragged from his meal. With a twist and a roll, Zayn's huge body pinned Spencer. Their tongues brushed, giving Spencer a new prize to suck. Zayn's hand found its way inside Spencer's pants. It was his turn to fight for release. It felt like Zayn was everywhere. Their kiss stayed passionate, but Zayn tugged Spencer's cock, teased his balls, and tickled his asshole. Spencer's attention was split. He didn't want to stop kissing, but his body strained. Spencer didn't know which sensation to focus on. Zayn decided for him by slithering down Spencer's body and licking Spencer's dick. Spencer clutched Zayn's shoulders and held on while Zayn gave a repeat performance of his last show.

The level of talent Zayn possessed was that of a professional. Zayn obviously wasn't someone who felt obligated to blow anyone. This was a man who did this out of a love for the sport. He deep-throated like a porn star and bobbed like he didn't need air to survive. Spencer's hips kept chasing Zayn's mouth, trying to get more. His ass automatically clenched as pleasure overcame him. The first spasm hit, and Zayn's name tore from his throat. His body bowed. He felt something he never had before. Spencer couldn't put a name to the emotion. All he knew was he wanted to hold Zayn as the last wisps of ecstasy still burned through him. He tugged Zayn higher and bit his bottom lip, demanding entry. Zayn's weight squished him, and Spencer welcomed it. The way Zayn's chest felt against Spencer's gave Spencer life. He wanted to crawl beneath Zayn's skin and touch his soul. More than anything, Spencer wanted to stay right here. He didn't want to do anything else or be with anyone else. It was an addiction-like craving for more. He didn't doubt the madness would pass. But for now, Spencer wasn't going anywhere. Spencer had found heaven. He intended to stay.

FOUR

THE HAPPINESS THRUMMING through Zayn had him walking in the clouds. Spencer left his laptop in Zayn's car. He was starting to wonder if all this forgetfulness was purposeful. Zayn was on his way to see Spencer again. Returning the man's property... again. He didn't think it was a coincidence. After all, Zayn had pretended he hadn't seen the laptop until he made it home earlier in the day. Maybe Spencer had done the same. He waited until after he snagged a few hours of rest until he headed back to Spencer's. Zayn wanted to make sure he had enough energy for anything Spencer might want to do once Zayn got there.

. . .

As Zayn climbed from his car, the warehouse door opened, and Spencer stood waiting. As usual, he didn't wear a shirt. His expression looked wicked as Zayn closed the space between them, as if he relished the thought of what he would do to Zayn. Zayn had to take a breath to stop himself from smiling like an idiot. He had never felt this way. Spencer owned his every thought. He wanted to be cautious. It was too late.

The moment he was within striking distance, Spencer snagged the hem of Zayn's shirt and hauled him inside. "There he is." That was all the conversation they had before Zayn found himself in Spencer's arms. Spencer had Zayn's jeans unzipped and unbuttoned before Zayn's ass hit the couch. Spencer straddled his hips. Zayn lost himself in the gluttony of being the center of Spencer's attention. No one had ever treated him like he was irresistible, the way Spencer did. It was thrilling—like he rode the highest of highs. Zayn was overwhelmed by the fantasy that maybe he could hang on to this dream forever. Part of him wanted to slow things down and talk about where they were headed. Most of Zayn was terrified he wouldn't like what he heard. He didn't imagine Spencer was the type to get tied down. All Zayn could do was take what he could get and hope for the best.

Spencer massaged Zayn's erection. "Tell me you want to fuck me as badly as I want you."

"I want to fuck you. It's all I think about." It wasn't a lie. Since the first time Zayn saw Spencer, he had been obsessed. He didn't know how to shake him.

A chime sounded and Spencer tore his mouth away from Zayn. Zayn licked the shell of Spencer's ear, hoping to keep his attention.

"Fuck. It's Jinx. I forgot he was stopping by tonight to drop off a new speaker to replace one that blew last night." Spencer climbed from Zayn's lap, pulling a whimper from him. "Don't move. I'll cut him off before he makes it inside and then you can get inside me."

• • •

Zayn tried not to pout. "Make it fast or I'm starting without you."

At his threat, Spencer rushed to the door. Zayn watched him until he couldn't see him anymore. When his voice came through a speaker, Zayn's gaze moved to a nearby monitor. He realized the chime had come from a motion sensor and the entire parking lot was under surveillance. He watched Spencer cutting Jinx off before he made it inside.

"Hey, man. I'll take that. No need for you to waste your day with me."

Jinx's head turned toward Zayn's car before looking Spencer's way again. "Isn't that Zayn's car? What's going on there? I've never seen you with the same person twice, much less three times."

Zayn caught himself leaning closer to the screen and hanging on every word.

. . .

Spencer made a dismissive motion as he moved the box Jinx delivered closer to the door. "There's nothing to tell. You know me. I'm just passing the time. Zayn is like a cute, over-enthusiastic puppy. I'll send him on his way when I get bored."

Zayn's eyes fell closed. He took a breath and then stood. He kept his mind blank as he fixed his clothes. Maybe he was naïve for thinking Spencer cared at all, but he wasn't weak. Zayn wasn't looking to be anyone's plaything. He headed for the door. Without glancing Spencer's way, Zayn slipped past him and made his way to his car.

"Whoa. Hold up, Zayn. Where are you going? I thought I told you not to move."

With his heart on lockdown, Zayn glanced Spencer's way. With one foot in the car, he tried not to break. "I'm not really in the mood to anyone's over-enthusiastic puppy tonight. You should find someone else to entertain you until you get bored. In fact, maybe you should get Jinx to take my place. I get the feeling he's interested in the job."

Zayn was too angry and hurt to even notice how his words were received. It was as if his brain had stopped functioning properly. He had been less insulted by the doctor looking to see if he'd had work done than this bullshit. Zayn couldn't believe he had let himself get taken for this ride. He pulled into Koda's driveway before he realized he didn't recall leaving Spencer's or the drive to Koda's. There hadn't been a conscious plan to go to Koda's. It was like his car had taken him where he needed to be. Zayn didn't question it. He climbed from the car and headed for the door. As he rang the doorbell, Zayn took several calming breaths. He didn't want to dump on Koda.

"Yes?"

Zayn tried sounding upbeat as Koda's voice came through the intercom. "It's Zayn."

. . .

"Hey. Just give me a second."

Zayn patiently waited while trying to put a lid on his raging thoughts. Koda opened the door with his son Liam in his arms. Liam threw himself forward at the sight of Zayn. A happy-sounding squeal pierced his ears.

Zayn smiled as he caught the toddler. "Hey there, buddy. How are you?"

Koda took a step back so Zayn could come in. "Sorry about that. He's grateful to have a break from me, I guess."

Zayn pressed his lips to Liam's forehead and inhaled. He needed Liam's unconditional love. "Don't apologize. I'm always happy to spend time with my favorite guy. Sorry for stopping by unannounced."

. . .

Koda headed for the couch, using his sight cane to avoid Liam's million toys. "It's no problem. We were just hanging out. I definitely could use a break from listening to the same cartoon playing for the millionth time."

Rather than joining Koda on the couch, Zayn sat on the floor with Liam and played with whatever Liam brought to him. He took a moment to calm down, focusing on Liam before trying to broach his need for Koda's company. "How do you and Felix do it? You make marriage and having a family look so effortless. As far as I can tell, no one is interested in building a family anymore."

Koda leaned his elbow on the arm of the couch and looked thoughtful, as if he took Zayn's question seriously. "Honestly? It looks easy because it is. We fell in love and neither of us fought it because we wanted it."

It was as he feared. Love was easy. It was just that no one wanted to build that with him. "Oh." His throat swelled. Zayn swallowed past the pain. "It's hard being considered extremely smart when you're really dumb as hell."

Koda leaned over and rubbed his shoulder. "Tell me what's happened, and we'll figure it out together."

Zayn watched Liam play while wondering if he had the courage to admit he had dreamed bigger than he should. He didn't know if Spencer had made him look like a fool, or if he had done that all on his own. Either way, Zayn was an idiot. A big dumbass who craved love. How stupid could he be?

Sommerland Music Group was a nondescript building not far from the warehouse district. Spencer had visited the place many times over the past twenty years. Having been in his twenties himself, Spencer had been beyond impressed by the twenty-year-old who started the business: Felix Sommerland. Like many people in L.A., Felix had come from money, but he used his good fortune to start a business that paved the way for several lucrative careers. Felix had seen more talent come and go than most. He had a great ear for perfection, and none of that had anything to do with why Spencer found himself there now. Felix was his friend.

As he pushed his way through the door, Spencer half expected Felix would be too busy to see him. The rest of Spencer questioned why he had come here at all. For the first time in his life, Spencer was confused about his feelings and questioning some things. He didn't know who else he could talk to about it. Felix was happily married to the love of his life. He looked like an actual adult to Spencer. That was something Spencer would never be.

Instead of being greeted by Felix's receptionist, Spencer ran into Felix as he stepped inside.

Felix did a double take, obviously surprised to see Spencer. "Spencer. Hey." Felix changed directions from heading for his office to greet Spencer at the door. A bright smile stretched his lips. He shook Spencer's hand. "Why do you always look homeless?"

Spencer glanced down at himself. His tank top had a hole in it. Plus, it was inside out and backward. He hadn't noticed. Spencer shrugged. "My head is always somewhere else. Why do you always look so put together? Aren't toddler dads supposed to be run ragged?"

A happy-sounding chuckle rumbled from Felix's chest. He motioned for Spencer to follow him and spoke over his shoulder as he went. "I have an amazing husband who does a majority of the chasing while I get the easy job of coming here every day. What brings you by?" Felix asked as he chose a seat inside his office.

Spencer plopped down in the first chair he came to. "What do you think of Jinx?"

. . .

Felix blinked, as if that was the last question he expected to be asked today. "The sound guy who worships the ground you walk on? I guess, I think he's good at his job."

Fuck. Everyone saw something he didn't. "Why would you say he worships me?"

A humorless smile touched Felix's lips. "I'm an expert on watching someone from afar while knowing they're so far out of my reach, they may as well be the stars. Jinx looks at you the same way. Hopeless romantics can spot other hopeless romantics a mile away. What's got you asking about Jinx all of a sudden? He's been working with you for years."

Spencer shrugged. "Someone pointed out that Jinx is interested in me this morning as they were storming out. Now I'm wondering if I'm a bad person because A, I never noticed, and B, I said something incredibly stupid to drive away the person storming out."

. . .

"Does this person have a name?"

"I'd rather not say."

Felix's eyebrows rose. "So it's someone I know."

"It's Zayn."

Spencer hadn't thought Felix could sit any farther back in his seat, but—somehow—he managed. It was as if his spine melted. "Damn."

Felix's reaction made Spencer even more nervous. "What? Why are you saying damn?"

For a moment, Spencer didn't think Felix would answer. Finally, he blew out a sigh. "Well, that's a rock and a hard place. If you had asked me if there was anyone who watched you with more hunger than Jinx, I would've said Zayn."

. . .

Spencer experienced a sudden burst of happiness before reality smacked him back down. He had just sent Zayn running. "Fuck."

"What did you say to send him storming out?"

It took every ounce of Spencer's will not to squirm in his seat. He scratched the side of his nose while avoiding Felix's stare. "I might have said something about him being an over-enthusiastic puppy I was only keeping around until I got bored." Spencer winced as the final word fell from his lips. Felix groaned, and Spencer couldn't leave it at that. "For what it's worth, I didn't think he would hear me."

Felix sat forward like he fought the urge to jump to his feet. "And that makes it better how? If you're using the guy, is it better to know or not? Fuck, he's still the one who gets hurt."

. . .

"I thought we were using each other." His claim came out much louder than intended, but Spencer didn't enjoy being a bad guy.

"Who were you saying this to for him to overhear it?"

"Jinx."

Felix stared at him without blinking—like Spencer had broken his brain. "I didn't think it could get worse, but there it is," Felix said after a moment.

Spencer's heart sank. He dropped his gaze to his feet. His eyes fell closed. He had on two different shoes and hadn't even noticed. Spencer didn't understand why anyone would want him for more than a night. He was pretty much a tragedy. Spencer was nowhere near the typical gay man. He never matched or had an ounce of style. Spencer was lucky if he made it out of the house fully dressed. He had the attention span of a gnat when it came to anything outside of music. Even his own mom didn't talk to him.

Spencer stood. "Thank you for talking this through with me. I hope fucking your friend over doesn't affect our friendship. I wasn't thinking."

Felix's shoulders fell. He looked defeated. "Spencer. Stop. We've been friends for over twenty years. I know you well enough to know you wouldn't purposely hurt anyone. Zayn is amazingly forgiving. I imagine if you made even the slightest effort to make things right, he would let you."

Even though Spencer nodded along, he didn't know if there was anything he could say that Zayn would believe. He would think about it. Maybe he would come up with a way to apologize. Even if he found the words, Spencer didn't think Zayn would talk to him long enough to hear them. He couldn't blame Zayn. Spencer was pretty dumb. Chances were good he had seen the last of Zayn. That was depressing.

It was the craziest peace offering. That was what Zayn kept telling himself to explain why he currently sat in the parking lot of a pottery studio. He was still angry and hurt, but now he was also intrigued. After spending a few hours with Koda and Liam, Zayn had come home to a simple note from Spencer. It said, "I'm sorry that I suck at a lot of things, but I'll always try new things with you." He had included a receipt for a pottery class in Zayn's name. It started tonight. The craziest part was, he had always wanted to try pottery-making. It was on his long list of hobbies he wanted to learn before he died. More than anything, though, Zayn was here because of one word in that note: always. Spencer had said he would always try new things with Zayn.

Since Zayn was a nervous mess, he waited until five minutes before class was set to start before heading inside. By the time he walked through the door, everyone was already seated behind a pottery wheel. He spotted Spencer slouching in a chair across the room. There was an empty station beside him. Zayn chose the one across from him instead. Spencer smirked as Zayn sat. Zayn looked away and focused on their instructor.

Despite paying attention the entire time, Zayn was still hyper aware of Spencer. Even as they dove in and learned by hands-on experience, Zayn kept checking Spencer out on the sly. He looked completely focused on the vase he was making. With his bottom lip between his teeth, Spencer seemed genuinely intent on learning the process. Zayn kept fighting back smiles. He couldn't make himself stop wanting this one person. At some point during the four-hour class, they managed to make passable vases and Zayn forgave Spencer. He was also a little disappointed to learn they wouldn't be taking their creations home yet, and the classes were spaced out several weeks apart. Zayn wanted to remember the experience.

As they stood to leave, people chatted happily with their parties as they headed out. Zayn dragged his feet. He didn't know if he was ready to talk to Spencer again. Zayn decided to let Spencer choose. Spencer fell into step beside Zayn as they walked to the parking lot, but neither of them spoke. He stayed at Zayn's side all the way to Zayn's car. Zayn's lights flashed as the door automatically unlocked as he approached. Spencer opened the door for Zayn. "Thank you for showing up. I would've stayed if you didn't, but it was better because you were here."

Zayn wanted to nod and get in the car without saying a word. He couldn't. "Thank you for setting this up. I've always wanted to try my hand at pottery-making. It was fun."

A bright smile lit Spencer's face. "Right? I half expected clay to go flying across the room, but it didn't and—" Zayn kissed him, cutting Spencer off mid-speech. It was out of his control. He needed to taste the excitement flowing from Spencer.

Spencer's hands flattened against Zayn's chest and slid upward. Zayn shuffled closer as Spencer's fingers found their way to Zayn's hair. He tilted his chin higher, getting as close as he could to Spencer as Spencer deepened their kiss. He recognized this might be the last time they touched. Zayn was okay with that since they would part on a happier memory. Even when the kiss ended, neither of them moved away. With their foreheads pressed together, Spencer kept his eyes closed as if savoring the moment while Zayn couldn't stop staring at him. He looked so normal tonight in his brown t-shirt, light-colored jeans, and work boots. It was like Spencer had attempted to fit in for Zayn. Zayn didn't want that, but it was sweet.

Suddenly, Spencer backed away as if he forced himself to take a step back. "Would you like to have breakfast with me tomorrow?"

Zayn fought a smile. "I'd love to, but I have a business meeting in the morning."

Spencer nodded, looking crestfallen. "Oh. Okay."

A chuckle rose and stuck in Zayn's throat. He couldn't help it. Happiness had him in a chokehold.

"There are other meals in the day. How do you feel about me cooking dinner for us tomorrow night instead?"

Spencer's smile returned. "I'd like that."

"Six?"

"Sounds good." Spencer looked around as if he didn't want to leave, but he knew they couldn't stand in the parking lot all night. "I guess I should let you go home."

"Yeah. I have that early morning thing. You probably have—" This time, it was Spencer cutting him off with a kiss. It was every bit as sweet as the last one. They were kisses with a promise behind them. Hope built in Zayn's chest. Spencer didn't kiss him like a man bent on fucking him until he got bored. He kissed Zayn like they had all the time in the world together. Zayn couldn't wait to find out if that was true.

FIVE

TRUTH BE TOLD, Spencer hadn't expected Zayn to show up for the pottery-making class. He had thought about Zayn looking to try something new, since the bodybuilder thing had gotten old. With that thought in mind, Spencer had taken a chance. Honestly, Spencer wasn't good at making amends. Since becoming an adult, he had chosen to live his life unapologetically. This time, though, he had been completely at fault. He needed to make things right.

Zayn had shown, and now he was making Spencer dinner. He hadn't expected to be under Zayn's roof again. Not only was he there, but he also had a club soda in hand and Zayn didn't seem to mind Spencer being nosy as fuck.

Spencer hadn't explored Zayn's place the last time he had been here. They had gone straight to bed. Afterward, he had sneaked away as quickly as possible. Now he couldn't stop inspecting everything. Zayn lived in the coolest house Spencer had ever seen. Everything was open and glass. Water gushed over the glass wall of the living room, fascinating Spencer. He tried tilting his head and leaning closer to the windows to see why.

"What's above us?"

"The second-story pool."

At Zayn's response, Spencer's curiosity tripled. "Do you have a leak?"

. . .

Zayn laughed as he moved to a nearby wall. "No. It's a waterfall. The water from the second-floor pool pours into the pool down here and is pumped back to the top again. The two are connected. See." He pushed a button, and the water stopped falling, clearing the view. They were literally standing in the pool. Spencer imagined it was only an illusion, but it was amazing. He wondered how the house looked from a distance with an endless pool of water flowing from one floor to the next. Zayn pushed the button again, and the waterfall resumed.

"Holy shit. That's amazing. You would think a waterfall would be loud, but I barely hear a thing."

"The glass is basically the same stuff they use in commercial aquariums. You know, the places where you can go see full grown sharks and whatnot." Zayn motioned toward a small doorway at the opposite side of the room. "If you head through that door, you'll find the indoor part of the pool. You can slide open the wall to swim through the waterfall. You can see how thick the glass is when you open it. It's like ten inches. It's soundproof and bulletproof."

. . .

Bulletproof? Damn. Spencer couldn't fathom Zayn's life. It had to be wild being this rich. "You have the coolest things. I can't imagine having even half of this."

A line appeared between Zayn's eyebrows. "It's not like you're poor."

Spencer sipped his drink and shrugged. "Honestly, my place is paid for along with everything else I own. Otherwise, I have about a hundred grand in the bank."

Spencer fought a smile at the way Zayn tried valiantly to hide his shock. "Are you not charging people for your work?"

A laugh burst from Spencer. "Of course I am. Money just isn't that important to me. I like to have enough in case of an emergency or whatever.

Otherwise, I try to improve the world around me. I have scholarships set up at two different music academies, and I keep the art program in several schools funded. Jinx's mom is on dialysis and can't afford it, so I pay for that. Plus, I keep up with her other bills, so she's not stressed. There are tons of ways I can help and still not struggle, so I do."

If Zayn felt one way or another about anything Spencer said, he didn't show it. Instead, he kept asking questions. "What about your parents?"

Spencer's muscles automatically tensed at only the mention of his parents. "What about them?"

Zayn shrugged. "You take care of Jinx's mom. What about yours?"

He fought the urge to say what he wanted. That she could go fuck herself. "I'm sure she's fine." After all, she could find any man she wanted to keep a roof over her head. Just like she had done his whole life, especially at his expense.

For a moment, Zayn stared at him expressionlessly, but he didn't push. Spencer wondered if there would ever come a day when he didn't look like the worst person on the planet to Zayn.

Spencer looked around for a place to set his drink. "Maybe dinner wasn't a good idea." He should have been happy with Zayn's goodbye kiss and left things at that. It wasn't like he would be any good at a relationship.

"Why?" Zayn sounded damnably calm. His peaceful tone made Spencer feel irrational. Zayn's reaction made him stop and think, which was something he didn't take a lot of time to do usually. Still, he didn't know how to answer that question.

Zayn crossed the room and took Spencer's drink from him. He set it on the nearest flat surface before towing Spencer into his arms. Zayn was strong and peaceful. It was mesmerizing. "You don't have to talk about anything you don't want to with me. Just tell me you don't like dredging up certain things. That's fine. I'm just trying to get to know you. This isn't an interrogation. I'd much rather you tell me to mind my business than to have you run away." He kissed the corner of Spencer's mouth. "Stay. Tell me happy stories."

Spencer kissed Zayn, hoping to stay in his arms. Even though he was taller than Zayn, Zayn was huge. He made Spencer feel safe. Spencer didn't feel quite so much like he was bumbling through life when Zayn wrapped his arms around him. He tried to think of a happy story for Zayn. Nothing came to mind. He didn't think Zayn wanted to hear about the new set list he made, and that was all Spencer had going on. Spencer realized something. Just as Zayn claimed he was boring; Spencer was dull too. He wasn't jet-setting or meeting new people every day. There weren't any exciting moments to share. He woke up every day and worked on his art. No one wanted to hear about that. Spencer buried his face against Zayn's neck and admitted as much.

. . .

"I don't think I exist outside of music. You don't want to hear about that nonstop."

"Yes I do."

With a laugh, Spencer took a step back. "You say that now, but you haven't spent years listening to me drivel on and on about how I found a new mashup."

Zayn didn't crack a smile. He looked completely serious. "That's exactly what I want. I should check our food."

As Spencer watched Zayn walked away, a million thoughts and emotions washed over him at once. Zayn was literally a billionaire. He could afford a thousand chefs, yet he cooked for Spencer. Zayn claimed to be interested in Spencer's work. Spencer had only been around people who told him he talked too much about himself—like talking about his music made him vain. He swung wildly between wondering if this was an act and hope. Spencer dangled in disbelief. With his mind raging with itself, Spencer wandered into the kitchen. One of four ovens stood open. There was a pan of food on the floor, and Zayn had his head on the counter with his hand under running water. Spencer dashed across the room, grabbed a potholder, and started picking up the mess.

"Holy shit. Are you okay?"

Zayn didn't lift his head. "Yeah. I'm just dumb as hell."

Spencer dumped the hot pan in the opposite sink. Zayn's fingers were red, and the skin already bubbled in three places. Spencer didn't try touching him. He pulled the phone from his back pocket and called a friend. Thankfully, Seth answered on the second ring.

. . .

"Dr. Black."

"Hey, Seth. It's Spencer. I need your help."

Seth didn't let him down. "You've got it. Are you home?"

Spencer shook his head, as if Seth could see him. "No. I'm at a friend's house and he's burned himself pretty badly. Can I text you the address?"

"Of course. I'm on my way."

Spencer tried to stay calm as he disconnected the call and quickly texted Seth the address.

"Are we just friends?"

· · ·

Zayn's question might have felt heavier if Spencer hadn't been in panic mode. "Yes, but I'm hoping you'll forgive me for being stupid so we can be more. Who do I need to talk to so the doctor can get onto the property?"

Zayn still wasn't moving from his spot on the counter, and that worried Spencer more than he wanted to admit. "There's an intercom on the wall by the waterfall control panel. Press the button and ask for Rocky. He's the head of security."

Spencer quickly moved to follow Zayn's instructions. He didn't know how long it would take Seth to get here, but he didn't imagine it would be long. He pushed the button Zayn described. "Hey, Rocky. We have an emergency."

A dude who matched Spencer in height and Zayn in muscle appeared from nowhere like a goddamn ghost, sending Spencer's heart racing into his throat. He was hard-looking and didn't as much as blink as Spencer grabbed his chest.

. . .

"Goddamn. Where did you even come from?"

The dark-haired and green-eyed man didn't waste time answering him. "You said there was an emergency."

Spencer nodded. "Zayn burned himself pretty badly. I have a doctor on the way. Zayn says you're the guy to make sure he can get onto the property."

"What's the guy's name?"

"Seth Black."

With a nod, Rocky headed for the door. "I'll make sure he finds you."

. . .

Spencer headed back to the kitchen, feeling confident Rocky would take care of things. Zayn wasn't leaned over the counter any longer, but his hand was still under the running water. Spencer moved to stand at his side.

He stared at Zayn's burns. "Damn. Burning yourself is the worst." He rubbed Zayn's back. "Seth will be here soon. He's a house-call doctor for the rich and famous. I've never used his services, but I know he's well-respected. We went to high school together." At this point, Spencer was just rambling. He couldn't stop. Being nervous always took hold of his tongue. "I know he's passionate about helping people. In fact, I would trust him with my life. He was always the one who took care of me when my mom's latest man would beat the shit out of me because they were bored. If he can deal with all that trauma with no medical training, he'll have you patched up in no time. This one guy, Buddy, hit me across the back with a cast-iron skillet he had just pulled out of the oven. It was a mess, but Seth fixed me right up. He'll have you out of pain in a hurry."

. . .

"Spencer?"

Spencer kept rubbing Zayn's back and playing with his hair, trying to soothe him. "Yeah?"

"Don't tell me anything else. I'm in too much pain to kill anyone right now, and I really do have enough money to get away with murder."

A smile exploded across Spencer's face. It was ridiculous. He shouldn't be smiling, but he couldn't help it. "I'm a nervous talker. You scared me."

Zayn's sexy gaze moved Spencer's way. He held Spencer's stare. "I wasn't thinking when I came in here. My mind was locked on you and how I can convince you I want all of you. I took the pan out of the oven without an oven mitt. It was a good thirty seconds before I realized I was holding a hot pan."

.   .   .

Spencer winced.

Zayn wasn't finished. "You're all I think about. I want to be with you."

"You are with me," Spencer said—like a dumbass—in his confusion.

A smile exploded across Zayn's face. "As a couple."

"Oh." Spencer would have thought he would need to think about it, if he had ever imagined this moment. That was not what happened. "I thought we were already a couple."

"Show me what's happened," Seth said, appearing inside the kitchen with Rocky hot on his heels.

Spencer stepped out of the way and let the blond doc do his thing. His head was oddly empty, considering everything so far today. He chewed his bottom lip and tried to keep all the thoughts at bay. For once, he wouldn't self-sabotage. Spencer was determined in that. He had met a good man. Zayn deserved to have a man who worked to be with him. Rocky openly stared at him, cutting through Spencer's shock.

Spencer held his gaze.

One of Rocky's dark eyebrows rose in challenge, and it hit Spencer. He was being silently threatened. Zayn had a staff that cared. If Spencer hurt him, Zayn had a staff that would hunt him down. Spencer smirked, because he was no one's bitch. Plus, he had no plans to hurt Zayn. They were a couple now. Maybe Spencer hadn't been expecting a relationship, nor had he wanted one, but Zayn was his now, nonetheless. No one would hurt him, especially Spencer. He would prove he wasn't his mom. Once and for all.

To Zayn's surprise, his hand didn't hurt that much. That was mostly due to Dr. Black and his amazing medicine bag. He hadn't made Zayn go to the hospital, but the pharmacy had delivered some cream and pain pills. Zayn felt like complete shit for ruining their dinner.

"I'm so sorry about our food. Grab my phone and order us something."

Spencer stuffed another pillow beneath Zayn's arm so it would be elevated. "I already ordered us something. Stop worrying over it. You have no idea how often I hurt myself because my head is always in the clouds. I've got this."

Zayn couldn't stop staring at Spencer. He had learned more about Spencer from this accident than he might have in ten years otherwise. He hated Spencer's past but adored the man he saw now. Spencer had claimed he wanted Zayn's forgiveness. He already had it. Every passing moment they spent together, Zayn saw a little deeper into Spencer. He wanted him even more for it.

"You're amazing. Really. You should get told that every single day."

A sexy smile stretched Spencer's lips as he settled in next to Zayn on the couch. "I think you're a little high."

Zayn shrugged and leaned into Spencer's side. "Maybe, but that doesn't change the fact that I'm speaking the truth."

Spencer touched Zayn's chin and tilted his face up, bringing Zayn's gaze to his. "You're gorgeous."

An insane desire to blush overwhelmed Zayn. "So are you."

. . .

Spencer leaned back a hair and inspected Zayn's face. "Are you blushing? Adorable."

Even more heat exploded through Zayn's face at Spencer's words.

A sexy, deep chuckle vibrated from Spencer. "I love that you're obviously not used to being complimented. That means I get to be the one constantly telling you how hot you are."

"I think you should kiss me." Zayn needed Spencer's kiss like he needed his next breath.

Spencer's gaze dropped to Zayn's mouth. "I think you're right." He dipped his head and touched his lips to Zayn's. It was a sweet kiss, but there was nothing innocent about it. Zayn swore he could feel Spencer's barely contained desire. He fought the urge to pounce and demand more. Instead, he let Spencer lead.

. . .

"Sorry to interrupt. This just arrived."

At Rocky's appearance, Zayn reluctantly pulled away. Rocky had six pizza boxes. "That's a lot of pizza."

Spencer sat forward. "I didn't know how many people you have on staff right now."

Zayn's chest warmed. He looked Rocky's way with his eyebrows raised.

Rocky set the pizzas on the coffee table. "There're five of us on duty tonight."

Spencer handed four of the boxes back to Rocky. "These are for you guys. They're all the same."

Rocky seemed reluctant to accept, but he didn't argue. "Thanks." He didn't sound thankful. Zayn looked at him closer, but Rocky didn't meet his gaze. "I'm sure the guys will demolish this in no time." Without a backward glance, Rocky headed out with the pizza.

"That was nice of you."

Spencer shrugged off the praise as he flipped open the lid of the box. "Since you burned your dominant hand, I figured pizza would be the easiest thing for you to eat."

Zayn shook his head. He didn't understand why Spencer didn't realize how amazing he was. People didn't visit his house and worry about his staff. Hell, they didn't even worry about him. Zayn puzzled over it while they ate. He didn't solve anything. In fact, between the food and the meds, he caught himself dozing. He closed his eyes for half a second. When they opened again, their mess had been cleared away, and Spencer was helping him to his feet.

. . .

"Come on, sleepy head. You obviously have a low tolerance for pain medicine."

Zayn let Spencer lead him to the bedroom. "I rarely take any type of medication. I come from an Asian family. My mom thinks capsaicin fixes everything."

A sexy chuckle rumbled from Spencer as he helped Zayn strip down to his underwear. "I get the feeling you have a great family."

Zayn dutifully climbed into bed when Spencer pulled the covers back. "They're good people. My mom doesn't love that I'm gay, but she doesn't bother lecturing me. I think more than anything she's worried about me getting mistreated."

"You're her baby." Spencer sat on the edge of the bed at Zayn's hip. "Good parents don't want their kids getting bullied. I imagine it has to be somewhat terrifying to send your kids into the world under the best of circumstances. Being gay definitely doesn't make anything easier."

"Are you not staying?" He didn't look like he intended to crawl beneath the covers with Zayn.

For a moment, Spencer eyed him in silence. "Do you want me to?"

He didn't need to think about it. "Yes."

Spencer stood and stripped. Zayn enjoyed the show. He knew in his heart they wouldn't make love tonight. Spencer struck Zayn as the type of person who never took advantage of anyone. The way he talked about taking care of others and the way he had thought about Zayn's staff tonight, that was a man with a moral code. He fascinated the fuck out of Zayn.

. . .

Spencer stacked pillows under Zayn's arm again and then circled the bed. He crawled beneath the covers and moved as close as possible without hurting Zayn. "I can't promise I'll sleep."

Zayn hadn't thought about the time. He realized too late it was probably still pretty early in the evening. "I'm sorry. The meds are making me tired, but you don't have to stay. I don't even know what time it is."

"It's about eight thirty." Spencer brushed his fingers through Zayn's hair. "That's not what I meant, though. I always have a hard time sleeping. Between working mostly at night and the way my mind races, I have a weird sleep schedule. I usually just go until I crash."

"Sounds like ADHD."

Spencer blinked, as if Zayn spoke a different language. "Not that I know of."

· · ·

Zayn closed his eyes and savored the way Spencer played with his hair. "My best friend growing up, Lonnie, had ADHD. He couldn't tolerate the meds, so he had to just deal with it. Lonnie would just go and go, playing video games, talking, playing different instruments, and basically anything else you can think of to pass the time. It felt like he was always moving or talking until boom. He would be asleep. Then he would stay asleep for hours on end. He was very creative."

"Where is Lonnie these days?" Spencer spoke softly —like he tried to lull Zayn to sleep.

Zayn fought a wave of pain. Some things never got easier to carry. "He killed himself our senior year of high school."

"I'm sorry to hear that."

Zayn fought the urge to say it was okay. It had been over twenty years. He didn't think about it that much anymore. Those were all the usual sayings for whenever anyone asked about Lonnie. This one time, he stayed silent and accepted Spencer's comfort. The pain meds were making him emotional. He was glad Spencer was here. Even if Spencer didn't end up staying the night, Zayn had Spencer for now. He was grateful.

SIX

SPENCER: *How is that hand today?*

Zayn: *It's good. How are you?*

Spencer: *I'm good. I'm just missing you.*

Zayn: *I'll be there in a few.*

Spencer: *Don't forget we have that second pottery class tonight.*

. . .

Zayn: *I'll be there.*

Up beats, downbeats, and echoes swirled through Spencer's mind. He moved to his DJ controller and opened his laptop. He pushed buttons and twisted knobs, lining up different sounds. Spencer moved to the sound, getting into the music and imagining people rocking out to his latest tracks. One new song led to two. He found a fresh memory stick and started a new set. There were three shows coming up that would be perfect for testing out his latest creation. A chime pulled him from his thoughts. Spencer's gaze shot to the security camera. Zayn's car pulled into his usual spot. Spencer's gaze slowly moved to the clock. His eyes fell closed. Pottery class had ended nearly an hour ago.

He bent at the waist and softly beat his head on his standing desk before rushing to the door. Spencer yanked the door open, profusely apologizing before

Zayn could blast him. "I'm so sorry. Fuck. I'm such an idiot. One second, I had plenty of—"

Zayn overcame him. His mouth covered Spencer's, cutting off his apology. Spencer tore at the button on Zayn's jeans as he walked him toward the bed. At the edge of the mattress, Spencer pushed, shoving Zayn down. Desire burned in Zayn's eyes. Spencer forgot about his new set list and everything else in his life, except Zayn. When they were together, everything always fell away, turning Spencer into pure need. He straddled Zayn's body and dragged Zayn's white t-shirt up his torso. At Zayn's wrists, he twisted, turning the shirt into a restraint. He used the excess to tie Zayn's wrists to his wrought-iron headboard. Not a single peep of protest came from Zayn, ratcheting up Spencer's lust.

With Zayn's hands bound, Spencer slipped down Zayn's body, kissing and biting until he could strip Zayn's lower half. Once he had Zayn nude, Spencer stood and eyed his prize. Zayn was hard all over. He watched Spencer with a heat that nearly singed

Spencer's skin. Spencer held Zayn's stare as he stripped.

"You are perfect." He tossed away his final piece of clothing and found the lube and condoms. "I would never forget about you on purpose."

Zayn didn't respond.

Spencer wondered if he was angrier than he wanted Spencer to know. It was okay. Spencer would fix everything. He crawled onto the bed and licked Zayn's cock. Zayn hissed. A smile tugged at Spencer's lips.

"You're so goddamn responsive. Since the first time I had you inside me, I've been captivated. No one looks at me the way you do—like you'd die if I stopped touching you." Spencer tore open the condom wrapper and slowly rolled it down Zayn's length. He purposefully tortured Zayn by not rushing. Spencer went to work on the lube next. He coated Zayn's length before moving to his balls.

"You make me wonder how far you'll let me go." Spencer met Zayn's burning gaze. He slipped his hand between Zayn's thighs and toyed with the spot underneath Zayn's balls. "How far will you let me go, Zayn?" Zayn still didn't make a sound as Spencer slid lower, but his legs parted. Spencer fought a triumphant smile. He circled Zayn's asshole with his lubed fingers. "You can't come yet," Spencer warned as he slipped a finger inside Zayn. A pant escaped Zayn. Spencer's cock leaked at the sound. He was turned on. Spencer wanted to sit on Zayn's cock and take everything he wanted. Instead, he couldn't stop tormenting Zayn. He curled his finger and pushed, massaging Zayn internally the same way he liked to be pleasured. Zayn squirmed. Spencer increased the pressure. Zayn's hips left the bed. Spencer snapped. In a flash, he straddled Zayn's hips and impaled himself. The headboard shook as Zayn fought against his restraints. He looked crazed as Spencer lifted and sat, riding Zayn's dick. Spencer held Zayn's stare as he used Zayn's cock while tugging at his own. Spencer let

Zayn see his lust and madness. He used Zayn's body. Spencer threw his head back and lost himself to the moment. He pictured himself crawling between Zayn's thighs. Spencer wondered if Zayn would let him push inside that tight ass. He loved the dick, but Spencer also liked to be the one pounding someone's ass occasionally. Zayn didn't seem like the type to take it. Maybe he would for Spencer.

"I'm not going to last, sexy. You're too hot and tight on my dick."

Spencer drew a ragged breath at Zayn's words. He dropped his chin and met Zayn's stare. "You'll come when I say so."

Zayn didn't look dominated. In fact, his expression said he knew exactly what Spencer wanted. "Finish me and then you're free to fuck me."

. . .

Something inside Spencer darkened. He needed to make Zayn see who was in charge. "I can fuck you now."

"Prove it."

A roar sounded in Spencer's brain. He leaped from Zayn's body and found another condom. After quickly suiting and lubing up, Spencer found himself on his knees, spreading Zayn's thighs and pushing his knees higher. He stared down at Zayn's asshole. It still glistened from Spencer's earlier play. Spencer wanted to shove his way inside. He couldn't until he knew how much he was about to hurt Zayn.

"Am I the first?"

"No."

. . .

At Zayn's answer, Spencer lost the final shred of self-control he possessed. "Thank god." He impaled Zayn.

A loud moan tore from Zayn.

Spencer took that as an oral agreement to go hard. He angled Zayn's body so every thrust would bring Zayn pleasure. His eyes burned as he fought to keep them open so he could watch Zayn's every reaction. Zayn's muscles strained, and the headboard creaked. An evil smile tugged at Spencer's lips. He wondered if Zayn would break his bed. Spencer kind of wanted to see it happen. Zayn's body bowed. Spencer's breath caught. He forgot everything but the sensations on his cock. Zayn's asshole squeezed him, making Spencer see stars. A strangled cry filled the air and then Zayn's body tried sucking Spencer deeper. A shout escaped Spencer as the pressure climbing his shaft turned into ecstasy. He rode Zayn's ass, trying to steal every spasm of pleasure. Spencer pumped the condom full of cum, wishing he could watch it leak from Zayn's asshole. Clarity hit harder and faster than Spencer's orgasm. He wanted more than he realized. While Spencer had admitted they were a couple, he hadn't thought about what that meant. Spencer recognized the truth now. He wanted this to be permanent. Spencer had zero desire to be with anyone else. He wanted a full-blown commitment where they didn't need condoms because there would never be anyone else. Fuck. He had found the one.

Zayn's body hummed with happiness. His wrists throbbed. He didn't care. All that mattered was the kisses Spencer kept letting him steal. He had started the night beyond pissed over getting stood up, but now he no longer cared. It wasn't as if he hadn't enjoyed himself at a class Spencer had gifted him. Plus, it was obvious Spencer felt like shit. In the grand scheme of things, one class wasn't that important.

Spencer held Zayn's hair and kissed him deep. Zayn took everything Spencer dished out. If Spencer was in the mood to dominate, Zayn was fine to hand over control. He liked this side of Spencer. When

Spencer finally settled down into Zayn's arms, Zayn's heart melted.

"I'd love to hear this new set list."

Spencer's head shot up. "How did you know it was a new set list?"

A laugh escaped Zayn. "Nothing else steals you away from me like music. Don't worry. I'm not jealous."

Spencer crawled until he settled between Zayn's thighs and hovered over him. "Well, I am. Where's that clay vase that stole you away from me?"

"We cooked them tonight. Next class, we paint them."

. . .

A frown marred Spencer's features. "You mean it'll be pointless for me to go to the next class since I missed this one?"

Zayn shook his head. "You're good. I convinced the instructor to let me cook yours as well."

Spencer's expression cleared. "That's good. I won't let you down again."

Before he could stop himself, Zayn released a loud sigh. "I'm not let down. It was an accident. I know you didn't ditch me on purpose."

Spencer groaned and pressed his face to Zayn's chest. "It sounds so terrible when you put it like that."

Zayn buried his fingers in Spencer's hair and scratched. "Maybe you can make it up to me by coming to a family cookout with me this weekend."

. . .

"Done," Spencer said with no clue how horrible it would be for him. Zayn's mom combined with Koda's entire family could be a real handful. Plus, this would be a declaration they were a couple. There would be no going back. His chosen family would want more of Spencer... just like Zayn.

As if Spencer read Zayn's mind, he licked Zayn's nipple. The breath caught in Zayn's throat. He felt Spencer's cock stir. "I've never been with anyone I can't get enough of, but I can't stop craving you."

Zayn's heart skipped a beat at Spencer's confession. He wanted more. "I'm not going anywhere, so take as much of me as you need."

"I don't think I have enough condoms to fill that tall order."

. . .

They were a couple. Zayn wanted them to be forever. He was happier than he had ever been in his life. "I'm sure we can find several ways to play that won't require condoms. If it makes you feel better, though, I have my doctor test me every year as part of my physical. Not only have I never slept with anyone without protection, but I also tested negative for everything right before our first time."

Spencer stared down at Zayn with a hunger that curled his toes. "Same to everything you just said. I've never let anyone touch me for any reason without protection. So tell me why I can't stop thinking about your cum."

Zayn's stomach muscles clenched with desire. He had never really been into bondage or cum play. Yet he wanted to try everything with Spencer. He needed Spencer's cum coating his tongue.

Zayn slapped Spencer's ass. "Flip around and sit on my face. You look like you need my dick in your mouth while I eat that ass."

. . .

"Goddamn." Spencer's hoarse-sounding whisper summed up Zayn's feelings as well. They were about to have a long night and would be sore in the morning. Zayn was ready for it. In fact, he was prepared to do this for the rest of his life. There was nothing he wanted more.

SEVEN

SPENCER: *I had a last-minute booking. It's for Saturday at noon.*

Zayn: *Oh, I thought we were going to that cookout on Saturday.*

Zayn: *It's not important, though. We can go anytime.*

Spencer: *Thank you. I'll make it up to you.*

. . .

Zayn: *I'll make sure you do.*

Spencer: *Why am I reading a ton of sexual innuendo in your text?*

Zayn: *Come see me and find out.*

Spencer: *I'm on my way.*

Spencer: *Don't let me forget our class tomorrow night.*

Zayn: *Okay.*

Zayn: *Don't forget our final pottery class tonight.*

Zayn: *I'm sending you the reminder you specifically asked me to send about our pottery class.*

Zayn: *I'm here. Where are you?*

Sweat glistened on Spencer's skin as he loaded the box truck by himself. He knew he could wait for Jinx, but Jinx's mom hadn't been doing well the last time he talked to her. Spencer didn't want to burden Jinx with extra work. His next show wasn't until tomorrow night, but if he finished this now, they wouldn't have to do it in the morning. That only mattered because the show was a two-hour drive from here.

"Hey. Why didn't you wait on me?"

Spencer flashed Jinx a smile as he came through the door. "I was just trying to get a head start. Honestly, I didn't mean to load everything by myself. I got carried away."

Jinx pulled a face, as if Spencer confused the hell out of him. "Don't you have some dumbass pottery thing or something tonight?"

Spencer's head shot toward the clock. He leaped from the back of the truck. "Oh, fuck. Fuck. Fuck. I'm so stupid. How did I forget again?"

Jinx laughed. "If you're smart, you forgot on purpose. Who in the hell takes a pottery class?"

Spencer didn't hear a word. He was completely in his head. Why did he keep forgetting these classes? Goddamn. It was like he didn't have a brain. Spencer ran for the door without looking back. He was halfway across town before he took his first steady breath. Goddamn it. He hadn't even grabbed his phone. Shit. He was the worst. Spencer couldn't even text Zayn to apologize. He slid into the parking lot over two hours late. Spencer didn't slow to look for Zayn's car. He hit the door running. As he threw the door wide, an empty studio and a shocked instructor met his gaze.

"Can I help you?"

Confusion had Spencer eyeing the empty room. "Sorry. I thought the pottery class was tonight."

"It was." The middle-aged mousy woman pushed her glasses up her nose, looking aggravated. "Since tonight was the last lesson, class was only two hours. I'm afraid you've missed it."

Spencer's shoulders fell. "Damn."

"You're Mr. Wright, correct?"

. . .

Spencer nodded.

She gave him a once over as if finding him lacking. "Mr. Tanaka took your *unfinished* vase home with him."

"Great. I'm the worst boyfriend on the planet."

"Yes. Zayn does look unhappy."

With that set down still slapping his brain, Spencer walked away. His shoulders felt heavy as he headed for his car. Zayn put up with way too much. He drove to Zayn's house on autopilot. Spencer wasn't sure what kind of welcome he would receive. If Zayn was smart, and Spencer knew he was, he would slam the door in Spencer's face. More likely, Rocky wouldn't let him past the front gate. He was more than a little surprised when no one stopped him. At the door, a guy Spencer hadn't seen before let him in.

. . .

"He's in the living room."

Spencer didn't stop for any reason. Not even to introduce himself to the hundredth guard he had never seen. He had to get to Zayn before they tossed him out. As he cleared the living room door, he spotted Zayn. Shirtless and with one foot on the table, Zayn stared out the window at the pool. The waterfall wasn't going, leaving a clear view of the faux tropical paradise that was Zayn's backyard. There was a glass of whiskey in Zayn's hand and an open bottle on the table. There was quite a bit missing already from the bottle. Two vases sat nearby. One was brightly painted. The other looked barely passable. It made sense his vase would look as sorry as him.

"I'm a huge idiot."

Zayn glanced his way. A small smile passed over his features. "Hey, baby."

. . .

While Zayn had that patient look about him—like he planned to let Spencer slide again. Spencer couldn't let that happen. He crossed the room. "I don't even know what happened. One second I was loading the truck for tomorrow. The next, Jinx was there wanting to know why I wasn't in class. I'm such a fuck-up."

Zayn cocked his head to one side and eyed Spencer. After a moment, he set his glass aside and patted the spot beside him. "What do you think about learning how to make beer next?"

Spencer crossed the room and joined Zayn on the couch. He didn't know how to react. "I don't know if I'm cut out to learn new things. Obviously, I'm not very good at remembering to attend the classes."

As Zayn leaned Spencer's way, Spencer automatically draped his arm over Zayn's shoulders so he could hold him. He pressed his lips to Zayn's temple while Zayn explained. "That's why beer-making is so perfect. We don't need to take a class or anything. I can buy the stuff, and whenever you're here, we can work on it. There won't be any times for you to remember."

Spencer's eyes fell closed. He didn't deserve Zayn. Spencer swallowed past the lump growing in his throat. "I picked the pottery thing. It seems only fair for you to pick the next new experience. Do you even like beer?" After all, Spencer had never even seen Zayn drink before tonight.

"Not really, no."

A chuckle rose and stuck in Spencer's throat. He shook his head. "It still blows me away that you once claimed you're boring. You're funny as hell." He kissed Zayn's temple again. "I'm so sorry. Nothing matters more to me than your happiness. I'm sure it doesn't feel that way, though. You should kick me out."

. . .

Zayn twisted and pressed his lips to the corner of Spencer's mouth. Spencer took advantage and claimed Zayn's mouth. Zayn hadn't kicked him to the curb or even called him on his bullshit. Spencer felt like the luckiest bastard on the planet because he definitely deserved to be put on blast. He didn't understand why Zayn put up with so much from him. Spencer wasn't sure Zayn owed Spencer his forgiving nature. It had to feel like Spencer fucked him over on purpose, but Zayn never said as much. Spencer was an avoidance kind of guy. If Zayn didn't want to fight, Spencer was more than happy to keep pretending he didn't suck.

Zayn pushed until he straddled Spencer's hips. The taste of whiskey coated Spencer's tongue, sending him hunting for more. Maybe they could get drunk and fuck all night, then—hopefully—Zayn wouldn't remember how Spencer ruined the first half of the night.

"Sorry to interrupt, but there's a guy named Jinx out front who looks a hot mess. He says it's important he speaks to Spencer."

. . .

Zayn immediately climbed from Spencer's lap. The irritation flashing in his features wasn't lost on Spencer as he came to his feet. Still, Spencer knew Jinx wouldn't show up here for no reason.

"I'll be right back." Spencer tried not to see the way he hurt Zayn again, or the accusing look Rocky gave him as he rushed from the room, but the building sense of unease had him scurrying outside.

Rocky was right. Jinx was a mess. His hair stood in every direction and he had obviously been crying. Spencer knew without even having to ask. Jinx's mom was gone.

Zayn grabbed his bottle of whiskey and empty glass and headed for the kitchen. Rocky stayed hot on his heels. Since Zayn already knew Rocky was bursting at the seams with lectures, he did his best to avoid Rocky's gaze.

. . .

After abandoning his glass, Zayn turned up the bottle. He wasn't upset. Zayn couldn't explain how he felt. Unimportant seemed a good place to start. He was highly aware that he was dead last on Spencer's list of priorities. It hurt a hell of a lot more than expected, but he wasn't angry. Mostly, he was unsurprised.

"How much longer are you going to let this go on?" Rocky asked, obviously deciding he was finished waiting for an opening.

Zayn swiped at his mouth, wiping away the whiskey that lingered on his lips. "I don't know what you mean."

To his surprise, Rocky stormed from the room before stamping back in, carrying the vases Zayn brought home earlier. He slammed them down on the counter next to Zayn.

. . .

"Take a good look at this bullshit right here, because this is the rest of your life. This is what you have to look forward to. Unfulfilled promises and silent rage. You will always do everything alone while he can't finish what he starts and has random dudes showing up at your front door."

Zayn eyed the vases but didn't respond. Instead, he took another drink. He couldn't say Rocky was wrong.

Rocky moved closer and set his hand on Zayn's shoulder. He massaged. Zayn's throat swelled. He didn't want to listen anymore. Zayn had known Rocky too long. The man knew him too well. Rocky wasn't one to hold back when he had something to say. He was more like family than an employee. God knew his real family never came to visit. "I live here, Zayn. You can't pretend with me. I know you're horribly lonely and no one puts you first. This guy isn't the one. He's proven time and time again that you don't matter to him. He'll make sure you always feel alone."

· · ·

"As much as I hate that I'm making that statement look true, I have to go."

At Spencer's sudden appearance and statement, Rocky snorted and walked away.

Spencer didn't bother looking Rocky's way as he passed. He kept his gaze locked on Zayn.

Zayn looked away and took another swig of whiskey.

"I'm sorry."

Zayn nodded and set his bottle aside. Without looking Spencer's way, he opened the sliding cabinet that hid the trash can. He knocked the vases into the can, uncaring as they smashed. He shut the drawer and picked up his liquor. "You always are." Even Zayn heard the dead note in his voice.

. . .

"Jinx's mom passed away."

Zayn still didn't look Spencer's way. "Please pass along my condolences." He felt like the worst person on the planet, but he also couldn't help but wonder if Spencer would drop everything if it was Zayn's mother. Somehow, Zayn doubted he would.

Spencer didn't move.

Zayn finally met his stare. "Don't let me hold you up. I'm sure Jinx is waiting."

Spencer opened his mouth, as if he had more to say.

Zayn pushed open the hidden panel beside him and slipped inside his bedroom. He wouldn't keep Spencer from his life anymore. It was obvious Spencer had too much on his plate. If Zayn loved him, and he did, then the kindest thing he could do was lighten Spencer's load. So Zayn would remove himself from the picture. Even though it meant breaking his own heart, Zayn had to walk away. He was just some guy with too much time and money. Really, he was no one at all.

EIGHT

THE FUNERAL CAME and went with a feel of surreality. Jinx had opted for cremation and nothing felt good anymore. There was no happiness anywhere Spencer looked. Jinx was asleep in Spencer's bed because Spencer didn't know what else to do with him. Spencer spent his nights on the couch, texting Zayn without luck. He had canceled all upcoming shows until further notice, and—oddly—Spencer had zero desire to get back to work. Everything felt empty.

A small part of Spencer wanted to rage about getting dumped for something out of his control. Spencer knew that wasn't true, though. He had been driving Zayn away for the full three months they had been dating. Spencer couldn't believe Zayn had lasted that long. Of course, that didn't make it hurt less. Spencer's chest hurt all hours of the day, and he didn't care to do anything but wallow in the pile of shit he created. He had concocted about fifteen grand schemes to win Zayn back. All of them were just as likely to fail as the next. Plus, he wasn't sure if Zayn deserved to have Spencer as a plague upon his life. Fuck, Spencer missed him, though. He craved the late-night talks and the off-the-charts sex. Spencer longed for the sweet kisses on his neck when they cuddled. The same thought slammed against his brain a million times a day; if only he had made it to that final pottery class, then Zayn wouldn't be done. That was all it would have taken to save them was for Spencer to have put Zayn first one goddamn time. Now Zayn had no forgiveness left in him for Spencer.

The chime sounded on the security camera. Spencer's gaze shot to the monitor. Someone headed to the door carrying a huge flower arrangement. Spencer jumped to his feet and rushed to the door before the delivery man knocked and woke up Jinx. Jinx needed the rest.

To his surprise, as he stepped outside, he spotted Rocky carrying the flowers. "Hey," Spencer said, sounding confused even to his ears.

Rocky didn't return his greeting. "These are for Jinx. Zayn didn't know where else to have them delivered, but he sends his condolences." Rocky passed the huge flower arrangement Spencer's way and turned away, as if he couldn't leave fast enough.

Spencer set the flowers on the floor inside the doorway and rushed after him. "Hold up. I know you don't like me, but could you please pass a message to Zayn for me?"

Rocky barely spared him a glance. "Nope."

. . .

Spencer didn't give up. "Please? He's not answering my calls or texts."

"Take the hint."

Spencer fought a growl. "I know I fucked up several times, but I love Zayn. If there's any way I can make things right, I will."

A loud breath burst from Rocky, as if he was tired as hell. He tilted his chin toward the sky—no doubt seeking help from above—before turning back Spencer's way. "What do you know about Zayn's family?"

The question caught Spencer off guard, but he rolled with it. "Zayn says they're good people."

A bark of laughter escaped Rocky. "You don't know Zayn well enough to love him if you believe that's the least bit true."

. . .

Spencer searched his memories. He couldn't think of anything Zayn had done or said to make him believe his parents were awful. Spencer knew they were divorced, but Zayn hadn't said anything bad about them. "Zayn has always spoken highly of them."

Rocky rolled his eyes. "Zayn speaks highly of everyone. Seriously. Have you ever heard him say a single bad word about anyone? For fuck's sake, he had me bring flowers over here after everything that's happened." Rocky scrubbed at his forehead, as if battling with himself. Finally, he met Spencer's gaze again. "Look, Zayn is easily the nicest person on the planet. I'm head of his security." His eyebrows rose, and he obnoxiously looked at Spencer closer, as if those words should explain everything. Thankfully, he expounded because Spencer was lost as hell. "He hired me after I got busted stealing one of his cars. How crazy is that? He took a bum off the street and gave him a place to live and a good-paying job rather than throw me to the wolves. I could've slit his throat in his sleep and been richer than God by morning."

. . .

"But you didn't."

Rocky shook his head. "That's because it took me less than a day to see what you haven't bothered to notice in months. Zayn may be rich, but he has nothing. So, no, I won't help you join the brigade of people who claim to love him while leaving him empty. For fuck's sake, you stood him up on his birthday."

"What?" Spencer was pretty fucking sure he had not done that.

Rocky gave him a sharp nod. "Why do you think he invited you to that cookout at Koda's mom's place? It was his birthday, and he knew no one else would remember. He was right."

Spencer felt sick. He didn't understand why Zayn hadn't just said it was his birthday and he didn't want to be alone. Then again, he did. Zayn always expected he would get the bare minimum from people, and still everyone failed him.

"I can't know what he doesn't tell me." Even to Spencer's ears, it sounded like a poor excuse.

"You'd know a lot if you fucking asked," Rocky shot back. He swiped his hand through his hair. "Look, I think you care, but I also think his mom does too. That doesn't make either of you good people. If you really want to be with Zayn, you will, but I won't help you accomplish it. I want to see him with someone who gives as much as he does, and—no—I don't mean financially. Zayn deserves someone who makes him smile. I haven't seen him do that in a long time. If that's not you, then why in the hell are you wasting his time?"

"I swear I'm not trying to."

Rocky shrugged. "Then prove it." He left Spencer standing there, no closer to having Zayn back than when he woke up that morning. Spencer headed back inside, feeling defeated. Jinx was up. He had carried the flowers to the kitchen and was reading the card when Spencer found him.

His gaze moved Spencer's way as Spencer moved to join him. The tip of his nose was red, and his eyes were bloodshot. He flashed the card Spencer's way. "I owe Zayn an apology. You two would still be together if not for me."

Spencer wrapped his arms around Jinx and held on. "That's not true at all. I should've explained that you're like a brother to me and I should've shown up when I said I would. That's not on you." Spencer pressed his lips to Jinx's temple and held him tighter. He no longer knew which of them he comforted. Spencer had fought his whole life for everything he had, and he wouldn't lose Zayn without a fight. All he needed was a plan. He could do this.

Meat sizzled on the grill. Kids screamed and splashed in the pool. People milled around the backyard, playing games, drinking, and talking. Zayn sat in a lawn chair near the back door. Felix sat beside him, but they didn't talk. It was Zayn's fault. Everything hurt all the time. He swore he smelled Spencer's cologne and heard his over-the-top and larger-than-life voice booming throughout the party. A smile tugged at Zayn's lips. He could see Spencer showing up wearing a winter coat and no shoes. Goddamn. He had really fallen hard for a hot mess. Zayn hoped it went away soon. He didn't want this constant pain in his chest.

Another hint of Spencer's cologne washed over him. Zayn turned his head in its direction, even though he knew Spencer wouldn't be there. He froze as familiar fingertips trailed down his arm before being pulled away.

As Zayn looked on in shocked silence, Koda's mom, Elena, dragged Spencer from person to person, introducing him to everyone at the backyard barbecue. Zayn blinked, trying to clear away the illusion. Spencer was still there. For once, his clothes matched the season, and he looked perfectly normal. His jewelry was missing, and his hair was brushed. Zayn hated it. He also couldn't figure out what in hell Spencer was doing there.

Zayn fought against the pains in his chest. He hadn't expected to see Spencer today, especially not at his family's weekly backyard barbecue. In fact, he hadn't thought Spencer ever listened to a word he said when he talked about these gatherings. Much less had he known if Spencer recalled how to find the place. Zayn had no clue why Spencer would show up now. He knew Spencer had been here once, DJing Koda and Felix's son's birthday party before they started dating. However, Spencer hadn't bothered to come with Zayn the entire time they had been dating. Zayn didn't understand why Spencer bothered now. There didn't seem to be any logical explanation. Unless Felix had invited him. It made sense Spencer would show up for anyone and everyone but him. Plus, it was Koda's mom who was introducing Spencer to everyone, as if she had expected him to be here today.

. . .

Elena was like a second mom to Zayn. He had known she would show Spencer a motherly kindness Spencer had been denied throughout his life. That was one of the main reasons Zayn had wanted Spencer to come to these things. God knew it wasn't to meet his mom. Zayn's mom still played cards with Koda's uncle and pretended Spencer wasn't there. Thankfully, even though they weren't together, Elena still showed Spencer every bit as much as kindness as Zayn had hoped. Zayn couldn't help but smile as he watched her hug Spencer continuously— like he was one of her own. No matter how much it hurt, knowing they were over. It wasn't about him in that moment. He wanted Spencer to be happy. After all, someone should be.

"I have to admit, I never thought Spencer would settle down. Seriously. Not ever."

Zayn glanced Felix's way at the confession. He fought the urge to admit Felix wasn't witnessing it now. Zayn couldn't force his tongue to shape the words, admitting they were over. Instead, he went with the next best thing.

. . .

"Me neither."

Zayn went back to staring at Spencer with all the longing in his heart. Spencer looked his way, as if he felt Zayn watching him. Heat passed between them. Zayn had to take a breath. There was no way Spencer still wanted him after everything that happened.

Felix stood. "I think I'll go find my husband."

"Okay." Zayn couldn't blame him. It wasn't like Zayn was very good company today... or any day, for that matter. He never had anything to talk about. No one understood how conscious he was of literally having nothing to say. Unhappiness washed over him like a tsunami. With his gaze averted from Spencer, Zayn stood and headed for the door. No one tried stopping him. Halfway home, he decided he didn't want to go back to the silence. Instead, he changed directions and headed for town. It wasn't until he sat inside the same restaurant where everything started with Spencer that he wished he had gone home.

At a table catercorner to his, the same fucking obnoxious heart surgeon sat with some blond guy. The poor kid looked barely out of high school and obviously had no idea the shithead doctor took every man there. It was better to be lonely. Zayn dropped the money for his drink and a tip on the table and headed out. It wasn't like he was ever hungry anymore. In fact, Zayn couldn't recall the last time he had eaten. His phone buzzed on the way to his car. Zayn checked the face.

Mom: *Did you leave without your date?*

Zayn: *No.*

He turned off his phone for good measure. Zayn was tired of being available for people and things that weren't available for him. He drove home on autopilot. The moment he was inside the safety of his home and away from prying eyes, Zayn settled on his couch with his laptop. It was time to go somewhere. He hadn't traveled in a while. There was nothing stopping him from spending the next year or so seeing the world. He didn't know why he hadn't thought to just go before now. Zayn could see it all. Maybe happiness was out there somewhere, and he was missing it. A movement out of the corner of his eye caught his attention. Zayn turned to tell Rocky his plan.

"What do you think about..."

Jinx stood with Rocky at his back.

"You have a visitor," Rocky said unnecessarily.

Jinx gave him a small nervous-looking wave. "Hi. Sorry to drop by unannounced. I didn't have your number."

. . .

Rocky slithered away as Zayn sat forward and set his laptop on the coffee table. "That's fine. Come in. I've been meaning to check on you, but I don't have your number either."

Jinx moved farther inside the room. With his hands shoved in the pockets of his hoodie, he still tried motioning around the room. "You have an amazing place."

"Thank you. Would you like to sit down?"

Even though he moved gingerly, as if unsure of his welcome, Jinx still sat on the opposite end of the couch. "Thank you for the arrangement you sent. Mom loved getting flowers. She would've been thrilled."

A wave of fresh sadness washed over Zayn. His mom didn't have much to do with him, but it would break his heart if she passed. "I'm sorry for your loss. It has to be a nightmare."

. . .

Jinx nodded. "I'm definitely ready to wake up now." He shifted uncomfortably as he stared at a spot over Zayn's shoulder. "I dropped by to apologize."

Jinx's claim caught Zayn off balance. "For what?"

Jinx made another gesture with his hands in his pockets. "For everything, I guess. Mom was sick for a long time and had been getting worse for a while. I knew she didn't have much time left, and Spencer is really the only person I've had to lean on. When he started dating you, I guess I became a bit territorial. I don't know how to explain it, but it should've never happened. Spencer is just my boss, and I get I ruined your relationship. I'm just... miserably lonely, I suppose."

Zayn's throat burned. For a moment, he swore he looked at himself. "You didn't ruin anything. It probably looks that way. God knows I've felt like the worst person on the planet since I know Spencer probably thinks that leaving with you is why I'm done. It's not." Zayn glanced around, trying desperately to find a place to start. "It's... sitting in that goddamn pottery class alone when it was his idea to begin with. It's every time he made plans with me and didn't show. He booked a gig on my birthday when we had plans, for fuck's sake. I mean, I completely understand that he needs to make money, but I'm just..."

"Incredibly lonely," Jinx finished for him.

Zayn's shoulders fell.

They sat in silence.

After a few minutes passed, Jinx nodded toward the laptop. "Are you going on a trip?"

. . .

Zayn shrugged. "I guess. I'm always alone anyhow. There's nothing stopping me from being by myself in a new location."

Jinx looked around. "No offense, but your place seems cold as hell. I've been here five minutes, and I feel isolated as fuck. Don't you own a TV or something?"

A laugh burst from Zayn. "This is supposed to be my tranquil room. Would you like to see the rest of the house? It's not as quiet."

Jinx lit, and suddenly, Zayn didn't feel quite so alone. It hit him how young Jinx was and how horrible life was for him right now. Jinx needed a little distraction. Zayn's money was good for at least that much. He could afford to keep Jinx entertained for the day and his mind off his loss. Zayn could do that, and maybe he needed that too.

Spencer had taken a huge risk by showing up at Elena's place. He had been here once before when Felix's son had turned a year old. Of course, that day, he had been working, DJing the party. He hadn't really met anyone other than Koda's mom and Zayn that day. This time, he came with a new purpose—to bully his way into Zayn's life. Also, he needed to see for himself if Rocky's claims were true. They were painfully, horribly accurate. He had watched as Zayn sat alone in a crowd of supposed friends and family. Felix had been the only one to sit and talk with him, but not for long. Zayn's mom didn't appear to notice Zayn at all. Spencer had been aware of every single move Zayn made. He had known the precise moment Zayn realized he was there. Spencer had known the exact second Zayn left. No one told Zayn goodbye, asked why he was leaving, or acknowledged he was gone. Spencer could have left then. He hadn't. Instead, Spencer had stayed and talked to everyone and mentioned Zayn's name to every single person. He had made his presence known. They might have forgotten Zayn existed. Spencer reminded them.

He saved Hana for last.

. . .

"So, you are dating my son," she said the moment his ass hit the chair beside her.

"Yes, ma'am."

Her dark brown gaze moved his way and swept over him. She looked away. "You look like someone who'll disappoint the fuck out of him."

Despite her nasty claim, Spencer bit back a smile. She was probably only four foot eleven and ninety pounds. Mean things usually came in small packages. He shouldn't have been surprised. Plus, she wasn't wrong. Spencer had already disappointed him. "Most likely."

At his agreement, she snorted. "Is that why he left without you?"

. . .

She was blunt. Spencer could be too. "I'm surprised you noticed he left since you never acknowledged he was here."

"He's my son. He can find the chair beside me as easily as you did."

Spencer wasn't having that bullshit. "You're right. He's your son. You could've found the chair beside him but didn't bother."

Her narrowed gaze slid his way again. "If you have something to say, say it."

Spencer stood and pushed his chair in. "I've already said it. It was nice meeting you."

She released a short, humorless laugh. "Most people care what their future in-laws think of them."

. . .

Since he had already lost Zayn, Spencer didn't have to worry about that. He was free to say what Zayn wouldn't. "Since we've been together for months and I've never seen you until I sought you out, I'm not that bothered."

Spencer walked away, unfazed by the drama he started. Zayn would never admit that it hurt him to be ignored by the people he financially carried. Spencer didn't give a fuck about anyone's feelings. Since he had caused all the damage he could and Zayn was gone, Spencer headed for the door. He almost made it to his car before Felix chased him down.

"Spencer, hold up. What the hell is going on?"

Spencer kept his features blank as he turned Felix's way. "What do you mean?"

. . .

Felix made a wild gesture. "I mean, you show up here separate from Zayn and you two don't even speak before he leaves. What the hell?"

He could make an excuse and leave. Felix wouldn't stop him again. Instead, Spencer took a deep breath and said the first words that popped into his head. "None of you deserve him."

Felix blinked, as if Spencer's words were the last that he expected to hear. "Okay."

Something broke inside Spencer. He had been hobbled by the fact that he was a complete fuck-up. No more. Maybe everything was his fault, but everyone else had taken a swing at Zayn before Spencer got there to level him. The people in Zayn's life needed to know they weren't blameless. "When was the last time you called to check on him?"

. . .

"Never," Felix said, sounding as if the idea of it was beyond him. "We're not really close like that. He's more Koda's friend than mine."

That was fair. Felix had married into this. "Sorry. I'm just angry. I watched Zayn get ignored today by everyone but you, and I don't even know what to say. This is supposed to be... never mind." Spencer didn't know how to get his point across. Maybe he didn't have one. His family was terrible, so it was possible he didn't know how a normal family functioned. Possibly, this was it. "I should go."

"Okay." Felix sounded sad, as if Spencer had broken something else. He was on a roll lately, losing friends right and left. Spencer probably shouldn't have come here. He wouldn't again. Without looking back, he headed for his SUV. He had one more mistake to make. Spencer headed for Zayn's.

To his surprise, whoever the night shift guard was, he waved Spencer into the house without argument. Usually, whoever answered the door would point

161

Spencer in the right direction. This time, he only had to follow the sound of loud voices and laughter. He stepped inside Zayn's gaming room and froze. Zayn, Jinx, and Rocky all wore VR headsets and held controllers in each hand. They laughed and cursed one another as they battled virtually for whatever prize they saw inside their goggles. Spencer found the nearest chair and watched. Even though he couldn't see what they did, it quickly became obvious that Zayn and Jinx had teamed up against Rocky. They teased him mercilessly. There was a pressure in his chest that felt a lot like pride as he watched the scene unfold. For the first time in years, Jinx looked his age. Spencer knew that was Zayn's doing. Spencer startled as Zayn and Jinx yelled triumphantly in unison while Rocky groaned. As one, they took off their headsets. Their laughter died away as they spotted Spencer waiting.

Rocky set his gear aside before taking Jinx's and setting it beside his. He slung his arm across Jinx's shoulders. "Come on. I promised you dinner if you won. I always keep my word."

. . .

Jinx flashed Spencer a smile as he let Rocky steer him from the room. Spencer watched the pair until they were gone. Then his gaze slid Zayn's way. Zayn put their gear away. Spencer's throat swelled as he stared at Zayn. He wanted the happiness back. Spencer craved the intimacy they once shared. He didn't want Zayn's anger.

"Should I ask?"

Zayn flashed him a strained-looking smile over his shoulder. "Jinx came by to apologize for coming between us. I assured him it wasn't his fault and then I decided he needed a distraction from his loss."

Spencer swallowed, trying hard to keep breathing through the pain. "You're a good man." He swallowed again. Nothing he did seemed to ease the pressure growing in his throat and behind his eyes. "Truthfully, I could use a distraction from the loss too."

. . .

Zayn sat in the closest chair, as if Spencer's claim took out his knees. "I'm sorry. I guess you were pretty upset about Jinx's mom too. You were close to his family."

Spencer shook his head. "I mean, I was, but that's not what I meant. Losing you is what's killing me."

Zayn didn't respond.

Spencer couldn't stop talking. "I met your mom."

"How did that go?"

Spencer fought to keep his feelings from showing in his expression and tone. "She's not the worst."

A smile snapped to Zayn's lips at Spencer's answer. "She isn't the best either."

. . .

Spencer smiled. "Oh, yeah. She does not like me. You won't be getting her blessing." His smile fell. "Not that you need it, since you're done with me."

Zayn didn't say anything.

The pressure in Spencer's chest doubled. He couldn't leave. "I went to the doctor recently, and it turns out you're right. I have ADHD. It's funny that you knew that when no one else ever bothered to check."

Zayn shrugged. "It wasn't commonly assessed when we were kids. My friend just got lucky because he had a pediatrician who saw more cases than most."

Spencer nodded. Zayn still hadn't kicked him out, so he didn't go. "They gave me a choice to try taking meds or go without since I've made it this far in life. Since it's obviously affecting my short-term memory, I've decided to try the meds."

. . .

For a moment, Zayn didn't say anything. He opened his mouth to speak before closing it again, as if thinking better of it.

Spencer couldn't take it. "Say whatever you meant to say. I can take it. Most likely, I deserve it."

Zayn smiled. "It wasn't anything bad. I just started to say, if you don't like the way they make you feel, don't keep taking them on my account. Then I remembered that was dumb. There's no reason for you to do anything on my account."

"Why?" The question popped out before Spencer could call it back. It was too late. The floodgates opened. "I want to make you happy. No doubt it doesn't look that way, but I do. It's not your fault I'm stupid."

Rage flashed in Zayn's eyes. "You're not stupid. When you open your mouth, I expect you to talk about yourself the same way you'd speak to me. Would you call me stupid?"

Spencer blinked. He had never seen Zayn lose his temper. "No."

Zayn gave him a sharp nod. "Then you don't get to talk about yourself like that either. You are mine and I expect you to be treated with respect, even by you."

Spencer held his breath. He was like a deer trapped in the headlights of an oncoming car. The last thing he wanted to do was to hope, but he couldn't stop it from happening. He didn't know if Zayn realized what he had said.

"Well?" Zayn snapped when Spencer didn't respond.

"Okay." He dragged the word out, hoping it was the right answer.

· · ·

Zayn scrubbed at his forehead. "Why do you drive me insane like this?"

Spencer didn't know how to respond, especially since he was pretty sure the answer was that he was dumb.

Zayn dropped his hand and stared at Spencer. "I shouldn't have lost my temper when you left here with Jinx."

"I know you weren't mad about that." Spencer had to be honest. He knew he had been fucking up way before that moment broke them.

"Still," Zayn said, dismissing Spencer's claim. "It was bad timing for me to finally break. Jinx needed you more than me."

"That doesn't excuse the hundred times you needed me, and I was too busy."

. . .

They stared at each other in silence.

Spencer couldn't take the anger. "I will do better by you. No doubt you're tired of hearing empty promises from me, but I mean it. I love you. I don't want to lose you."

Zayn didn't react. He simply stared at Spencer in silence.

A humorless smile tugged at Spencer's lips. "Do you have nothing to say?"

"I usually don't," Zayn said, sounding calm. "But in this case, I'm thinking. Do you know what I think our problem is?"

"What?" Spencer needed Zayn to have the answers.

. . .

"I think because of your short-term memory issues, a lot of our problems are just an out-of-sight, out-of-mind thing. When we're not together, you don't think about me."

Spencer's eyebrows snapped together into a scowl. "That's not true. I think about you all the time."

"Were you thinking about me all the times you forgot about me?"

Zayn didn't sound angry, merely curious. That had Spencer truly considering the question and answering honestly. "No. Every time I forgot our plans, I was always distracted by whatever I was doing at the time. When I'm working, I lose myself to it."

"You should move in with me."

. . .

Spencer blinked at the sudden proclamation. "What?"

Zayn nodded. "If you forget me because you're busy and you honestly don't want to do that anymore, then move in with me. I should think it would be pretty fucking hard to forget me if you're under my roof."

Spencer jumped to explain his initial reaction. He didn't want Zayn to get the wrong idea. "I'm thrilled at the idea of sleeping in the same bed with you every night. That's not the issue. I don't want to give up everything I own for someone who doesn't love me."

A line appeared between Zayn's eyebrows. "You don't have to give up anything, and of course I love you. I wouldn't have suggested this if I didn't."

"Oh." Seriously, Spencer had nothing else. He hadn't expected Zayn to admit to loving him when he had been so thoroughly finished with Spencer only moments ago. Another thought hit. "I don't want to be another person in your life who takes more than they give."

"Then don't be." Zayn said the words as if the answer was that simple, and really, it was. Spencer could be here each and every day, giving Zayn the love everyone else denied him. The more Spencer thought about it, the more he wanted to stay here with Zayn.

"I've missed you so goddamn much."

Zayn dropped his chin as if Spencer's claim overwhelmed him. When he met Spencer's gaze again, he looked devastated. "I'll never forgive myself for letting you leave here to take care of Jinx alone. I should've been there for you to lean on. You have no idea how angry I am with myself."

. . .

Spencer shot to his feet and crossed the room. "No. We're not doing that." Spencer went down onto his knees at Zayn's feet. "We're new at this and I should've told you sooner that Jinx is like a little brother to me."

"He's so young," Zayn said, sounding surprised he hadn't truly noticed that sooner.

Spencer nodded. "He definitely needs us, but it's on me that I didn't say that. My point is, we're bound to make mistakes. We just need to start talking to each other instead of each of us waiting on the other to flounder through." He held Zayn's stare, needing Zayn to see his heart. "I love you. You're the man I want. I'm not perfect, but I think you love me anyway. We are too amazing together to let anything tear us apart."

Zayn traced Spencer's jawline, stroking his beard. "That's definitely true. Since the very first time I set eyes on you, I haven't stopped thinking about you.

There isn't a doubt in my mind the universe has been driving me toward you. I am so, so in love with you."

Spencer's eyes fell closed at the confession. He had been closer to losing Zayn for good than he ever wanted to be again. "There's nothing I won't do to keep you."

Zayn touched his lips to the corner of Spencer's mouth. He lingered, sweetly teasing Spencer with the lightest of kisses. A breath caught in the back of Spencer's throat as desire stirred in his gut.

"I want you," Zayn whispered against Spencer's lips.

Spencer's body hummed with need.

Zayn wasn't through torturing him. "I've been slowly dying without your hands on my skin."

. . .

"What about Rocky and Jinx?"

Zayn scrubbed his fingers through Spencer's beard again, nearly rolling Spencer's eyes back in his head. "Rocky took Jinx out to dinner. That was their bet."

Spencer was on his feet in an instant, towing Zayn out of his chair. He didn't look back to see Zayn's reaction as he rushed Zayn through the house to Zayn's bedroom. The moment they were closed inside, he fell on Zayn like a crazed fiend. Their hands were everywhere, tugging and pulling. He heard fabric rip. Spencer was beyond caring. In a show of sexy strength, since they were both big guys, Zayn lifted Spencer off his feet and tossed him onto the bed. Spencer bounced and then sank into the luxurious mattress. Zayn's features were hard as he stripped away the bottom half of Spencer's clothing. All Spencer could do was gasp for air and take it.

Zayn barely had his dick out and the bare minimum of lube applied before Spencer's legs were over Zayn's shoulders and Zayn cock was in Spencer's ass.

There was nothing sweet about their coming together. It was primal and desperate—just like them. They were carnal people, and their sex life had always been phenomenal. Tonight was no different, except now there was a desperation in the air. They had almost lost each other. That tinted everything. There was a blush of promise in their encounter. It was dark and possessive. Spencer clawed at Zayn's skin, trying to pull him deeper. Zayn's hold was bruising as he pounded inside Spencer. Cries and gasps filled the bedroom. Monstrous desire clawed at Spencer's brain. Pre-cum leaked onto his stomach as pressure climbed his shaft. His open mouth gasped for oxygen as he strained toward release. Spencer held Zayn's intense stare. The first spasm hit. A cry ripped from his throat as cum shot from his dick, hitting his bottom lip. Spencer swiped it away with his tongue.

Zayn roared as he slammed his hips against Spencer's ass. Even as ecstasy lit his skin ablaze, Spencer couldn't stop watching Zayn as he pumped Spencer's ass full of cum. He couldn't wait to be left leaking. Spencer felt owned in that moment. He belonged to someone. Zayn wanted to keep him forever. Spencer's eyes burned at the thought. He gasped for breath, but for a new reason. Spencer fought the tears that tried escaping. He had been so close to losing the only person who loved him. His whole life, he had been unwanted. Now this beautiful man had asked to keep him. He was vulnerable in a way he had never been. Spencer felt like they were part of an epic love story. One where the fuck-up won the popular guy. He never wanted to wake up from this dream.

Their touches turned loving and their kisses sweet. Time passed as they snuggled beneath the covers, touching and kissing while whispering words of love. As Spencer drifted to sleep with Zayn in his arms, his hold automatically tightened. Never again would he let Zayn slip away. Zayn was stuck with him.

NINE

THE DINING ROOM smelled like bacon and eggs. Zayn savored the way Spencer played with his fingers beneath the dining room table. It felt strangely right to have Rocky and Jinx at the table, enjoying a peaceful breakfast with them. They felt like a family. Zayn's chest swelled at the thought. He wanted this. He didn't want to go back to living in silence and slogging through every moment alone.

"Spencer is moving in." The words burst from Zayn. He hadn't planned to make any huge announcement or anything. It simply happened.

. . .

Rocky never looked up from his plate. He kept eating like it was just another day. "Sounds good. I'll make sure all the guys know."

Jinx was all smiles. "That's great. I'm so happy for you both. Seriously. It's amazing to see you both smiling."

Zayn wasn't finished. "Also, we were thinking, how would you like to join us, Jinx? There's plenty of room here."

Jinx's jaw dropped.

Zayn kept going, pleading his case. "There's enough space in this house that you could see as little or as much of us as you like. I know I'm asking a lot, but we enjoy having you around and I don't like the idea of you being alone right now."

Spencer squeezed his fingers beneath the table.

. . .

Zayn didn't dare glance his way since they hadn't talked about this at all. It had been a spur-of-the-moment decision. Jinx was young and alone in the world. He was a genuinely sweet guy. Zayn couldn't send him home to be alone with his dark thoughts after losing his mom.

Jinx glanced around the table, visibly grasping for anyone to help him deal with Zayn's offer. Rocky was all about his food, proving his life wouldn't be affected either way. Zayn tried to keep his expression hopeful. Jinx's gaze landed on Spencer and didn't move.

Spencer didn't let Zayn down. "Seriously, Jinx. You've always been like family to me. We want you here with us. Plus, I'll likely be working from here once I find a spot in the house to set up. It would be easier for you to be here than to make this drive every time I have a gig."

. . .

Jinx's eyes softened. His shoulders relaxed. "Okay. Yeah. I mean, if you two promise to tell me if you get sick of having me underfoot, then yeah. Wow." He looked every bit as blown away as he sounded, and Zayn knew he had made the right decision.

"You have a guest."

At the sudden interruption, Zayn glanced over his shoulder to find his mom standing in the doorway. Zayn fought through his shock to stumble to his feet.

"Mom. Hey. I didn't know you were stopping by. Would you like some breakfast?"

Hana glanced around the kitchen, taking in the people at the table. "Good morning, boys. Maybe I'll join you for a small bite. Spencer, Zayn, and I have plans to meet Elena and her boys for lunch today, but a few slices of bacon shouldn't hurt."

. . .

Zayn tried clinging to reality as he held a chair out for his mom to sit. There was so much to take in, Zayn didn't know where to start. He hadn't known about any plans with Elena. It was possible she had told Spencer since he had been at Elena's yesterday, but Zayn doubted it. Zayn reclaimed his seat at Spencer's side. He sat in a shocked haze while Hana introduced herself to Jinx. Spencer squeezed his fingers beneath the table again, somewhat pulling Zayn from his daze. Zayn noticed Rocky still stared at his plate, obviously trying to stay out of everything.

Hana wasn't having it. She lightly smacked Rocky's arm. "Hey there, boy. How have you been? Have you been staying out of trouble?"

"Yes, ma'am." Rocky barely muttered the words before excusing himself from the table. Zayn understood. Rocky had always been super protective of Zayn. By extension, he didn't care for anyone he felt took advantage of Zayn. That included Zayn's mom.

. . .

The moment Rocky was gone, Hana turned Zayn's way. "You did a great thing by giving Rocky a job. He's a good boy."

Zayn nodded. He was still trying to figure out what train had hit him. Slowly, Jinx and Spencer disappeared to do different things, leaving Zayn alone with his mom. She wasted no time once they were alone.

"It's funny. Until I spoke to Spencer yesterday, I thought I was doing right by you."

Zayn didn't know what he was meant to say to that. He chose the bare minimum. "How's that?"

Hana made a helpless gesture. "You live this lifestyle that I don't understand. I never had money until you gave it to me. So, to me, I just imagined you out living some jet-setter life that I could only dream about having at your age. Instead, it seems you've been here, and I've been ignoring my only child. I honestly thought you wouldn't want an old lady in the way of enjoying youth, wealth, and all those things have to offer."

"And you learned all this from Spencer?" Zayn tried keeping up, but the shock kept his brain addled.

"Obviously, he wasn't cruel and didn't say all that, but he made me see I've been wrong." Hana took his hand between hers. "You are my baby and always will be. Every day, I wake up full of pride for the man you've become. I'll admit it was hard for me to accept that you're gay, because it felt like I was losing any chance of being a grandmother someday. Having Elena around helped when I learned your truth, and it's helping now that I see her with her grandchild. I've been wrong about a lot in my life, but I am here. I love you and I wish I could see you more often."

"Of course, Momma. I love you too."

. . .

She patted his hand. "Now tell me about Spencer and Jinx."

Zayn held his mom's hand and told her about Spencer moving in and Jinx losing his mom. He explained how he couldn't let Jinx go home to mourn alone. Before he knew it, two hours had passed, and he had talked more than he had in years.

Hana nodded along, interjecting occasionally until she noticed the time. "Shit. It's almost time to meet Elena. Get dressed and grab all the boys. Jinx and Rocky should go with us too. I should get to know Jinx so I can mother him, and Rocky has never liked me, but I'm not giving up."

Zayn kissed her cheek and moved to do as told. More than anything, though, he wanted to find Spencer and hold him. He didn't know what Spencer had said to his mom, but he felt like he had her back. Zayn could never thank Spencer enough for that. He didn't even know where to start.

Although Spencer hadn't expected Zayn's mom to come around because of anything he said, he had to admit it was amazing to see Zayn looking so happy. He also enjoyed lunch with everyone. However, Spencer's mood started to deteriorate about hour eight. He didn't mean to turn quiet, but everyone else was so loud. Usually, when Spencer was in a large crowd, he had music playing in his ears and could tune everyone out. That wasn't happening today. Spencer kept fighting back panic attacks. By the time they made it home, Spencer was ready to scream. Everything felt like too much. He wasn't used to so much busyness. Hana had agreed to play poker with Jinx and Rocky, making Spencer worry he was nowhere near the end of the tunnel.

Before he knew what happened, Spencer found himself inside a dark coat closet with Zayn holding him tightly. Quiet surrounded him. Spencer took a deep breath. Zayn didn't make a sound, proving he understood Spencer's inner panic. Spencer closed his eyes and held on while Zayn slowly rubbed in circles on his back. His mind calmed a hair.

. . .

"Tell me what you need from the warehouse and I'll send someone to get it." He pushed something on the wall inside the closet and a secret passage opened into a nearly empty room. "I'll have them bring it here and you can be alone for a while."

"How many hidden passages are in this house?" Spencer asked with a laugh as he stepped inside the room.

Zayn's eyes flashed with mischief. "Several. I'll show you someday. For now, you can have this room to work in or whatever. You need a break from me."

As much as Spencer wanted to feel like shit, Zayn made it impossible by being so understanding. Still, he needed to clarify one thing. "I don't need a break from you. There's just too much noise."

. . .

Zayn nodded. "You need to escape. Give me a list of what you need."

Spencer typed a list of necessary items from the warehouse into Zayn's phone. He gave Zayn the info he needed to get inside the warehouse and explained where everything could be found. Zayn nodded along. Once Zayn had all the information he required, he gave Spencer one last kiss and left him alone. Spencer eyed the lone chair and empty desk in the room. The room was pretty bare. There was nothing special about it, but it was quiet. Spencer checked out the closet and the connected bathroom. Everything looked unused. After he finished snooping, he sat and pulled out his phone. There wasn't a ton he could accomplish with only a phone, but he had access to his music files.

Time passed. Spencer lost himself. A guy who worked nights came and went, dropping off equipment. In no time, Spencer had his laptop and DJ board. With his headphones in place, he went to work. He moved to the beat in his ears without thinking. His mind calmed. Peace settled over him.

Spencer didn't think about anything. The world around him ceased to exist. He blinked and realized Zayn was there, sitting on a couch he hadn't noticed anyone bringing into the room. It was like that for him, though. He zoned out whenever he worked.

Zayn smiled when Spencer focused on him.

Spencer swiped his headphones back, uncovering his ears. "How long have you been sitting there?"

Zayn shrugged. "Maybe an hour. I like watching you work. Even though I couldn't hear the music, I swear I know which songs were playing by the way you move. Very sexy."

Spencer restarted the audio file, playing his new set from the beginning. Then he turned off his headphones and set them aside so the music filled the room. "Tell me what you think." As Spencer made the demand, he crossed the room. He straddled Zayn's lap so he could watch the emotions cross

Zayn's features while he listened. After three seconds passed, he decided he would rather taste Zayn's lips. They were too tempting to resist. When Spencer claimed Zayn's mouth, he tasted love. It was crazy that he had never been in love before Zayn, but he recognized it so easily. Spencer wanted Zayn to himself.

"Where is everyone?"

Zayn kissed Spencer's cheek. "Rocky is working. Jinx ran to his apartment to grab some things. Then he plans to pick out his bedroom. Mom went home two hours ago."

Spencer couldn't stop swiping kisses every time Zayn paused. Zayn was too irresistible. "Does that mean I have you to myself?"

"It does."

. . .

Spencer urged Zayn onto his side so they could cuddle. "Good. I vote we hide here for a while and snuggle."

He felt Zayn smile against his throat. Zayn's lips skimmed his neck. "Thank you."

"For what?"

Zayn held him tighter. "For being you. You talked to my mom and you've been taking care of Jinx for years. No doubt Rocky has tried intimidating you, but you don't show it. I love you. I never dreamed I could be this lucky."

Spencer massaged Zayn's side, dipping beneath his shirt so he could hold on to bare skin. "Don't thank me for doing the bare minimum. You're easy to love and I'm stubborn. I'm pretty sure I'll find some unique ways to fuck up."

. . .

He felt Zayn shrug. "Maybe I will too, but I think I was meant to meet you. So I'm not worried. This was written in the stars."

A smile tugged at Spencer's lips as his eyes slipped closed. He savored the sensation of Zayn in his arms while his music filled the air. The moment felt like magic. In his years of spinning tunes, he felt like he had brought a lot of joy to people. He was positive music made the world brighter. Spencer hadn't thought he needed more. Now, while holding Zayn, Spencer saw there were more ways to brighten his world. He had been missing a whole chunk of himself and hadn't known it. Until he met Zayn, Spencer hadn't realized there was another half of him out there. Now he would go to any lengths to hold on to this. Spencer had a new type of music to fill his soul. He had love.

TEN

FOUR MONTHS without his mom hadn't eased the tightness in Jinx's chest. Sometimes he wondered if he would ever feel normal again. He didn't know what would have become of him if not for Zayn taking him in. It wasn't that Jinx couldn't afford to live on his own. Spencer had always paid him well. It was a mental thing. Jinx didn't know if he could have lived alone with himself these past few months. Maybe he would have gone insane. Instead, there was always someone there, keeping him distracted. Hana mothered him. Zayn and Spencer were like brothers. Rocky... Jinx didn't know how to finish that thought.

. . .

Jinx's gaze slid Rocky's way. This was the first time Rocky had attended a rave with them. He told himself it was Spencer's talent combined with the sweet offer of being behind the scenes of one of Spencer's shows that brought Rocky here. After all, only the most elite guests were allowed to sit in the back of their box truck at the edge of the stage. It was prime seating at such a wild event. Only Jinx, Rocky, and Hudson were inside the truck with the best view. Since Rocky could watch Spencer do his thing while practicing at the house, Jinx wasn't sure that theory held water. Jinx wondered if Rocky was there because Spencer had decided he wanted Zayn on stage with him tonight, helping him with the new set. Rocky wasn't really a bodyguard as much as he was in charge of keeping Spencer's property secure. So Jinx didn't know if that explanation made sense either. Plus, Spencer and Hudson already had security surrounding the stage and truck, keeping them safe.

Hudson's hand slid up Jinx's spine. His lips touched the shell of Jinx's ear. "What are you doing after this?"

. . .

Jinx tried to keep his eyes from turning Rocky's way. He usually spent half the night playing video games and talking to Rocky. That was on normal nights, though. They would already be awake until nearly dawn by being here. "I'm not sure. Probably nothing."

Jinx swore Rocky watched them from the corner of his eye. He looked stiffer than usual.

On the sly, Hudson lightly kissed the spot beneath Jinx's ear. "You should hang out with me again."

"I'll think about it." Fuck. Jinx had never been more torn. On one hand, he already knew Hudson would rock his world. On the other... Jinx's gaze slid Rocky's way. Damn. There was something about Rocky. Butterflies stirred in Jinx's stomach when they were together.

Hudson winked as he jumped from the back of the truck and headed into the crowd. Jinx tried not to stare. He was well aware that Hudson chose him. Hudson could point to anyone at the rave and crook his finger. They would be bent over in a heartbeat. Yet Hudson picked him. Rocky probably never would. He got that Rocky was older than him and likely was only nice to Jinx because of Spencer. Jinx would be dumb as hell to pass on a night with Hudson, only to go unnoticed by Rocky. Nothing in his head made sense anymore.

"That guy seems to know you really well."

Jinx blinked. Rocky sounded harsher than Jinx had ever heard him sound. He didn't know what to think.

"Yeah. He hires us three to four times a year to do these raves. Nine times out of ten, he hangs out in the truck with me. I guess the partying bores him."

Rocky let out a bark of humorless-sounding laughter. "Yeah. I'm sure that's why."

. . .

Jinx stared at Rocky's profile, willing Rocky to look his way. "Do you have something to say?"

Rocky finally turned away from watching Spencer and Zayn. His features were hard until he focused on Jinx. Then his eyes softened. The breath caught in the back of Jinx's throat. Rocky shook his head. "You're so very young."

A spike of unexpected irritation raced through Jinx. "Maybe compared to you, old man, but I've been taking care of myself and everyone around me since I was twelve. So if I want to hang out with rock stars, I will. I'm not so young and dumb as to think anyone wants more than sex from me, if that's why you're shaking your head at me. I'm not stupid enough to think Hudson fucking Vincent will drop to one knee and ask anyone to marry him, much less a nobody like me." Jinx honestly didn't know why he was angry or what made him snap. Maybe he was a little pissed off that Rocky didn't see him as anything more than a kid brother. Fuck. This was doomed. He wouldn't keep seeking Rocky's company each night. Jinx had turned into a goddamn idiot.

. . .

"He'd be lucky to have you."

Confusion shook Jinx at Rocky's firmly spoken claim. They stared at each other. Neither of them spoke. Rocky took a step closer. Jinx's heart beat a little faster, making it harder to breathe.

"I hate to interrupt this blazing good time, but I want everyone to look at my sexy man, Zayn."

As Spencer's voice filled the speakers and the music lowered, Rocky turned away. Jinx swallowed. His gaze slid toward the stage. Spencer was motioning toward Zayn, showing him off like a showcase girl on a game show. He walked a circle around Zayn, as if eyeing a prize.

"Isn't he a beauty?"

. . .

Loud whistling came from every direction. Zayn looked like he fought the urge to cover his face.

Spencer was in rare form tonight. He always did his best performances when he was like this. Jinx's eyes widened as Spencer dropped to one knee.

A sexy chuckle rumbled from Rocky.

Jinx's gaze turned his way. His breath caught. Rocky was smiling. He was breathtaking.

"What do you say, Zayn? Do you want to stay on this ride with me forever?"

With his hands covering his mouth, Zayn nodded. Even with soundproofing surrounding them, the cheers were deafening as the adorable couple kissed. Jinx smiled and clapped, but a hollow pit opened in his gut. Life was passing him by while he stayed stuck in mourning. He knew his mom would want him to live his life and be happy. Jinx just couldn't shake this cloud that choked him. He fought the urge to look Rocky's way again. Maybe he was wasting his time here. Hudson was a perfectly good option. He didn't look at Jinx and see a child. Jinx was twenty-five, for fuck's sake. This entire situation was ridiculous. He would stay and let Hudson fuck him out of this dark mood. Rocky didn't want him. One dick was as good as another.

People milled around, finding their tents and yelling their congratulations. Zayn floated in a daze of disbelief. The past several months had been some of the craziest and happiest in his life. He had gone from spending ninety-seven percent of his time alone to having a house filled with people and love. It had been amazing. Never in a million years had Zayn expected Spencer would want to get married. Much less that he would be the one to ask... in front of hundreds of people, no less. Zayn couldn't stop smiling.

. . .

They lingered outside Zayn's Hummer. Spencer looked every bit as stunned and happy as Zayn. Spencer glanced over his shoulder at the vehicle. "I'm having a bit of déjà vu. Haven't we been here before?"

A hum rose in Zayn's throat. "Damn. That was an incredible night." He held Spencer's stare. "I think this one has it beat already, though." Zayn couldn't stop smiling. "I still can't believe we're engaged. You're amazing."

"Am I?" Spencer asked the question so nonchalantly —like he genuinely couldn't see what Zayn did. "Or am I mediocre and your love blinds you to it?"

Zayn took a step forward. Their bodies collided with Spencer pinned against the Hummer. "I love you more than life, but that doesn't blind me to shit. You're amazing."

· · ·

Spencer's stare turned sultry, making Zayn's mouth go dry. "You're so fucking sexy when you get bossy. Obviously, I always find you hot, but this side of you... damn."

"We should go home."

Spencer's expression turned wicked. "I mean, yeah. We could, but also..." Spencer tilted his head toward the back of the vehicle.

Zayn found his gaze dropping to Spencer's mouth. He knew exactly what it could do. In his mind, Spencer already had those sexy lips wrapped around Zayn's cock. "You should get in." Even Zayn heard the growl to his voice.

While Spencer scurried to do as Zayn demanded, Zayn headed for the back to turn the seats into a bed. It was by no means comfortable, but they wouldn't notice in a minute. If Zayn knew nothing else, he knew Spencer could transport him to another plane with only a look.

As he folded down the seats, Zayn caught another glimpse of his engagement ring. His breath caught. Zayn hadn't known this much happiness existed in the world. He stopped to catch his breath.

"Are you okay?"

At Spencer's quietly spoken question, Zayn lifted his chin and met Spencer's gaze. An overwhelming sense of coming home washed over him. "I'm perfect."

As Spencer crawled between the front seats and joined him in the back, Zayn recognized how true his answer had been. Life was absolutely flawless. There was no place else he would rather be or anyone else he would rather be with. His life was one hundred percent perfect. Zayn knew in his heart, as long as he was with Spencer, their lives would always be like this. This was forever for them. He couldn't ask for a better life.

Keep an out for the next Candied Crush, *Beautifully Torn*.

If you enjoyed this story, please consider leaving a review on the site where it was purchased. Reviews really help drive more interest toward my books, which allows me to keep writing. Thank you, Charity.

ABOUT THE AUTHOR

Charity Parkerson is an award-winning and multi-published author with several companies. Born with no filter from her brain to her mouth, she decided to take this odd quirk and insert it in her characters.

*Eight-time Readers' Favorite Award Winner

*2015 Passionate Plume Award Finalist

*2013 Reviewers' Choice Award Winner

*2012 ARRA Finalist for Favorite Paranormal Romance

*Five-time winner of The Mistress of the Darkpath

Connect with her online:

—Sign up for my newsletter: https://sendfox.com/charityparkerson

—Join my readers' group on Facebook: http://bit.ly/CharitysTribe

—Website: charityparkerson.com

—Facebook: facebook.com/authorCharityParkerson

facebook.com/TheMenofSin

—Twitter: twitter.com/CharityParkerso

—Instagram: Instagram.com/sinnerauthor

—Bookbub: https://www.bookbub.com/authors/charity-parkerson

—Amazon page: author.to/CharityParkerson

—TikTok: http://www.tiktok.com/@charityparkerson